THE PRODIGIOUS EARTH

finalist for the 2020 Noemi Press Book Award in Prose and long-listed for
the 2020 Dzanc Books Fiction Prize

also by the same author

Physically Alarming Men

THE PRODIGIOUS EARTH

Eric Blix

ERRATUM PRESS

ISBN: 978-1-7397708-4-6

First edition.

This book is a work of fiction. Any resemblance to actual persons, living or dead, are coincidential.

First published in 2022 by Erratum Press
Sheffield, UK
www.erratumpress.com

Design and typesetting by Ansgar Allen

CITY

[1]

In the Civil Defense Caves of eastern Idaho, near Grand Teton National Park, about a two-day walk to the Utah border, a family hunting for arrowheads were surprised to find a burlap sack containing human remains. Just a torso, no legs, arms, or head. Authorities had little information that could help them identify who this man might have been. They could tell he was an outlaw of the early twentieth century, killed in 1915 or so, by the old jail shirt and that, obviously, his life ended with an extravagant burst of violence. What seemed notable was the extent to which the mummification process had set in and preserved the corpse. Medical examiners at the University of Utah school of medicine were able to determine the presence of a foreign object lodged in the stomach. They cut it open and peeled back the layers of hardened tissue, surprised, perhaps just as surprised as that family hunting for indigenous relics, to discover the torso of a G.I. Joe action figure originating from a line released by Hasbro Industries in 1968. As one would expect, they could not easily explain its presence.

[2]

In *The Marvelous Clouds*, John Durham Peters tells us that "Ontology is usually just forgotten infrastructure." In other words, what we often take for natural grounds or systems are in fact constructions we no longer see or understand as constructions. Humans, who exist at scales that render such infrastructure invisible to us, operate therefore under conditions they cannot always, or perhaps ever, discern or comprehend.

Benjamin Robertson, Abstract to "Infrastructures of Horror,"
a talk delivered 31 January 2020

[3]

The Behavioral Health Unit was designed to promote therapeutic interactions of all conceivable varieties. Stan, like everyone, was not allowed to bring many personal items upon admittance, certainly nothing he could use to intoxicate or kill himself. And yet he could bring books. He began his stay with a series of German translations, starting with the John E. Woods edition of *The Magic Mountain* [this convinced him he both was and was not sick] and the Schocken edition of "The Metamorphosis," translated by the Muirs [this seemed to confirm the cruelty of his alien, carceral world], before crossing time to the New Germany, represented by W.G. Sebald's *The Rings of Saturn*, translated by Michael Hulse, and Jenny Erpenbeck's *Go, Went, Gone*, translated by Susan Bernofsky [who has her own version of Kafka's horror story], both of which thematically and formally concern themselves with the mechanisms of remembering and forgetting, the ultimate forms of mass destruction. After reading, he would lie in his cell, gazing at the sky through the lone window near his bedside, imagining the dissipating waves of old gunfire weaving like rose tendrils through the wire lattice. Somehow along the way, he got his hands on a copy of a novel by the Spanish physicist-poet Agustín Fernández Mallo titled *Nocilla Dream*, the first of Fernández Mallo's strange post-poetic network unofficially called the *Nocilla Project*. The book begins with a description of a solitary tree standing on the side of what Fernández Mallo, by way of *The New York Times*, calls the "loneliest highway in North America". The highway is officially known as U.S. Route 50, a transcontinental roadway spanning the North American interior from West Sacramento, California to Ocean City, Maryland. The truly lonely part is a specific stretch in the state of Nevada, where, after eliding Folsom [known largely for Johnny Cash's famous prison concert] and Lake Tahoe in the west, the highway connects Carson City to the empty desert surrounding the small town of Ely, just south of West Wendover and the salt flats at the Utah border. When John Bearheart picks him up and asks, Well now where in the hell do you wanna go… Stan tells him of the desert, of Fernández Mallo's temporary voyager, a discharged vet called Falconetti, who starts and later aborts a walking journey across the continental United States in defiance of Columbus's landing and everything it set into motion. It's an American tradition to go around in cars and look at remote places. They head west.

[4]

She always attracted the most complicated customers, the outlaw types who would pay a thousand dollars for a basket of onions, follow her upstairs, and tie her by the wrists, leaving her an hour later with bruises on her thighs. Most would return the next day or even that same night in tears asking if she'd marry them. They'd always do it the same way. Appear somehow on the property, pulling their cars up the drive or simply wandering there, perhaps after days in the Mojave Desert, and silently examine the girls behind the vegetable stands. These guys always seemed to manifest on the grounds without any real origin, always with a bottle in their hand, always tilting slightly and on the verge of finally weeping. Every time the same procedure, they eye the market up and down, pacing slowly from one end of the lot to the other, then back again, their slow footsteps kick up plumes of dust so faint they might not exist, three or four times up and down, up and down… They inevitably stop, step forward, and release a breath no one could tell they'd been holding in. It never fails. Every time it's the same. They look at the dust around their feet and follow her inside. So there's no wonder he does it this same way, like all the others. He maneuvers his car around the corner, a particularly tight and bosky hairpin known in the area for producing frequent crashes. He noses down the drive among red flowering myrtle trees and a simple wooden fence running along each side, passes under the overhead gateway of hewn oak logs, a bleached steer skull mounted in the center above the hanging sign for the Black Rose Gardens. The 64 ½ Mustang clicks and lets off heat after he kills the ignition and steps out. Earth crunches under his boot heels as he studies the produce on display. He might not yet be eighteen. His chin is solid and smooth and perfectly hairless. He chews on an unlit cigarillo and wears boots handmade inexpertly of the sidewinder's flesh, heels whittled from the primordial meat of the yucca tree. They all vividly recall the band on his hat, a strip of fur and skin wound around a chassis of rabbit bones, and his ghastly buckle, the whitened pelvis of a young coyote fastened to his belt. After this hybrid leaves, the girls all call him Billy the Kid. On his third visit to the farm, after much silent pleading, after small gaps in their talk lead him toward the door, she finally lets him stay the night. She lays on her back with her hands clasped beneath the pillow. He rests his head on her stomach and asks twice for her to stroke his shoulders thinking maybe her mind is on something else, either his simple request doesn't register or she ignores it. He tells her about his affinity for the sounds of the desert and the musical instruments he assembles out of local materials. He doesn't know from the outset what shape each instrument will take, what sounds it will produce, or how it will be played, whether he'll need to pluck a string, pound out rhythms on its surface, or pucker his lips and blow into a hole. I finished the Mojave last year, he says. Right now I'm working on the Sonoran, then the Great Basin. I'm still in the gathering phase. So far I've got four snake skins and a petrified wedge of what must be a calcite. I'm going down to Slab City tomorrow. I'm thinking I might buy some junk off the locals and work that in. You can come if you want. I'd really love it you came with me. Before he goes, they have one last beer in the downstairs cantina. They leave their glasses on the counter with rings of froth still clinging to the insides. She wishes him luck with his instruments. Maybe he'll bring her one when he comes around again. Next thing is the screaming muscle car, he whips it forward and tears out of the lot. The tumult wakes Silvia, a seventeen year old who bleaches her hair blonde, tends the rose bushes, and lies about her age. Below the window, she sees skid marks in the soil, dust lingering in the first creeping tendril of daylight. In the cantina, Billy the Kid left or forgot an indigestible sculpture, an assemblage of animal skins, desert stones, and a single tin cup fused by a silicone epoxy. Before breakfast, Silvia takes it into her room and sets it on the desk among healing fluorites, a framed Death card on which the flag-bearing skeleton rides its white horse through a field of the dead and dying, and an assortment of decorative skulls. She keeps it with her for the duration of her life at the Black Rose and for long after—a memento, or perhaps worse, a visual stalemate.

[5]

Beginning in 1940, before Pearl Harbor, scientific knowledge useful in war was pooled between the United States and Great Britain, and many priceless helps to our victories have come from that arrangement. Under that general policy the research on the atomic bomb was begun. With American and British scientists working together we entered the race of discovery against the Germans.

> Harry S. Truman, Statement Announcing the Use of the A-Bomb at Hiroshima, Hiroshima Prefecture, Japan [https://millercenter.org/the-presidency/presidential-speeches/august-6-1945-statement-president-announcing-use-bomb]

[6]

Whereas the human torso was placed into a refrigerated storage unit, no one quite knew what to do with the fragment of G.I. Joe. A medical student, a collector of action figures and other vintage toys, noticed that its shirt replicated the garment found on its human container in perfect detail, down to the shapes, colors, and textures of blood stains and mineral deposits, and was as such obviously custom made—though whether by an assembly line, a careful hand, a miracle of nature leaving its marks, or some interaction of forces was impossible to determine. Without consulting anyone, the medical student took the G.I. Joe torso to his apartment, stood it upright on the coffee table as much as it could remain so, and turned on a Roy Haynes record he had owned for several years but had not listened to until now. He watched the torso from his couch as if it was a television, long into the night, far longer than he had intended, deep into the static emitted from the speaker system after the record ended and the homogeneous crackling ensued. There's nothing that says a building cannot function analogously to a human body, nor that the human body itself cannot be conceived as a mobile housing module. The human species will go extinct as the doll infinitely reduces to its substrata of tinier and tinier microplastics. The downstairs neighbor, upset at the incessant static, pounded on the frontier line of ceiling and floor. In 1991 a girl uncovered a mummified hand in the Civil Defense Caves. Years later, forensic geneticists linked the human torso to a name. The head has not been found.

They were used to camera crews, because the local news affiliates liked to cover the automobile crashes that occurred on the corner at the end of the drive. It wasn't uncommon to turn in, coming back from L.A. or San Bernardino, and see a helmet-haired field reporter standing at the edge of the road, looking solemn as he or she faced the camera and narrated a tale of sudden tragedy. Silvia figured the crashes gave news stations and their audience something to be angry about, drunk drivers and texting behind the wheel and an indifferent or ineffectual city council, a production that allowed them to see and feel viscerally that their community was not immune to chance and atrocity. They'd even come around once to do a story about the Black Rose shortly after she had first started working there. A few of the older ladies said afterward that it was a semi-annual event, every two or three years one or another of the news stations would come around, interview everyone in the house, get some shots of the garden out back, and, even though everyone knew the Black Rose was really a brothel, produce a schmaltzy inspirational story about the young nuns of organic urban farming. Today two reporters arrived with their crews, one Anglo for the English-language NBC affiliate and one Chicano for the Spanish-language Corona-Los Angeles Telemundo station. They arrived back to back, parking their vans in a parallel formation where the Mustang had peeled out. They received no comment from two San Bernardino police officers, who were leaving after gathering statements from several of the Black Rose residents about their missing colleague. Once inside, the Anglo reporter and her crew trooped upstairs, probably hoping to ambush someone in their bedroom, while the Chicano reporter and his crew remained in the yard, capturing B-roll footage of the vegetable stands and house. The cops and then the Anglo woman both asked about the strange object on Silvia's desk. The cameraman wondered whether he could get it on film. Silvia thought for a moment and said okay. She posed beside it, ran her hands along its fur and edges, and gazed into the camera with real or simulated pride. Rafael asks about it, too, late at night. He yawns deeply and turns in the sheets and studies it from across the room. She runs her nails along his back, tracing her name in cursive. She tells him what she told the others, I made it myself. He asks what it means. It doesn't mean anything, she says. It's kind of like the crystals, I guess. It's a shape you can't name. They look at it for a while. The object inspires a game in which she scores secret messages on his back and asks him to say what she has written. She spells the same three words again and again, *Paul is dead*. He cannot guess them. He shivers and laughs when she tells him. As he fastens his belt, staring out at the sunrise, he asks one more time if she'll come along to San Francisco. I don't know, she says. You aren't like Billy the Kid, are you?

After the police and news crews left, she wiped the makeup from her eyes and lay in bed for most of the afternoon. She might have fallen asleep. At some point, she can't remember what time exactly, she changed into her work clothes and weeded the rose garden, sipping now and then from a frosty bottle of beer. A car pulled in, some old make and model she had never seen before, not even on television—a 1999 or '98 Peugeot cabriolet, a real pile of shit. A frumpy little man got out and approached the garden. She smelled his cigar well before he came shuffling around the corner, scratching his head with one hand and holding the other behind his back. He wore scuffed and unlaced desert boots caked around the soles in ocher mud, a khaki suit and green necktie with the knot loosened under his throat, and a rumpled raincoat even though it was sunny and the garden thermometer read 33°C. He seemed disoriented and maybe a little drunk. She wasn't sure if he noticed her, but how couldn't he, she was squatting twenty feet away from him in the open grass. He was still looking around and studying the place when he finally introduced himself. He was a private investigator, he said, working the Black Rose Murder [she had not heard either the police or news reporters refer to her missing compeer this way; like everyone, she had assumed the woman had simply run off with Billy the Kid, or that she was dancing in a club in Vegas, or that at worst it was a kidnapping and therefore she could be found]. He wanted to ask the ladies at the farm a few questions about their friend, this so-called Billy the Kid, anything they might remember about him or the events of that evening. No big deal, really, he was simply gathering statements from possible witnesses. I guess that means you, he said. He mentioned that he'd been to Slab City. He mentioned the way tilapia wash up on the mudflats when the Salton Sea ebbs and dries. The sun kills them and dehydrates their flesh. They remain exposed, their bodies warped and leathery, until the water returns and holds them on its surface, which is saturated with hydrogen sulfide and often smells like the essence of death.

[8]

Many people report the paranormal manifestation of faces in everyday objects. On 11 September 2001, moments after Flight 175 crashed into the South Tower of the World Trade Center, a contingency of witnesses [those fleeing from the wreckage on the street below as well as those watching on TV] claimed to have observed a face develop in the smoke billowing from the 70th floor. Their claims appear to be verified by a well known Associated Press photograph as well as footage from CNN's live feed of the disaster, since archived on the online video sharing platform, YouTube. Each apparatus, the photographer's and videographer's respective cameras, captured distinct patterns approximating eyes, nose, mouth, and chin. Some people believe the face resembled images of Satan typical of medieval painting. American president George W. Bush declared, *Today our nation saw evil.* Other witnesses and subsequent observers have claimed the face is an image of the terrorist, Osama bin Laden, his uncanny return in the fallout of his nefarious deeds.

Osama bin Laden was assassinated on 2 May 2011 at his compound in Abbottabad, Pakistan [named in January 1853 for Major James Abbott; headquarters of Hazara District during British Raj after annexation of Punjab; Wikipedia offers no name for the region before the presence of British colonizers]. His twelve year old daughter is said to have witnessed the event. To ensure the identity of their target, the American Military measured the corpse at 6 feet 4 inches [i.e. bin Laden's known height] not with a tape measure [they did not have one handy], but by requisitioning a Navy SEAL of identical height to lie beside it, then comparing the length of the living man to the dead one. They tested the corpse's DNA. They tossed it swiftly to sea. Some Americans cite the quick

DNA results and hurried sea burial as evidence of a staged spectacle, signs that bin Laden was not killed, and the very premise of his death is a hoax.

From *New York* magazine:

> Two UTEP computer scientists explained the face through "simple geometric analysis" of the physics of smoke-shapes after an explosion—a cone, horizontal lines.

[9]

For a few years back in the early 80's, behind the Golden Nugget Gambling Hall on the old Las Vegas strip, a secret fight club would meet once every month. They gathered beneath the neon tubes of Vegas Vic, that glowing cowboy pointing the way through the unreal nights, and together made their way to the Golden Nugget bar. They eased into their monthly affairs, fraternizing with drinks and stories because they were all Don Aurelio's men, a few of them cops as well, then they headed out to the alley, Don Aurelio's alley, where they threw down their bills, drew names, and brutalized the flesh. The Golden Nugget is famous for its appearance in the Elvis Presley/Ann-Margret feature, *Viva Las Vegas*, and its blurry background presence throughout a chase sequence in the James Bond film, *Diamonds are Forever*. In the lobby, a massive golden nugget called "The Hand of Faith," the largest ever found with a metal detector, named for its crude resemblance to the human appendage, draws tourists from the street, strip, and desert beyond, as if it is a shrine or a holy relic. These days a person can stop in the Golden Nugget gift shop or at any of the souvenir stands along the moving sidewalks and purchase a t-shirt of any color they wish featuring the glimmering image of the Hand of Faith on the torso, any golden t-shirt or those featuring Playboy Bunnies and Latin American revolutionaries and silhouettes of the Eiffel Tower, or in some cases commemorative "Never Forget" or "Where were you?" t-shirts in remembrance of the 9/11 terrorist attacks, though one wonders if the people who buy these connect 9/11 t-shirts with the fact that their fingerprints are collected and stored in a federal database or that their bodies are scanned and examined in the virtual nude before they are able to board the plane to their vacation in what Jean Baudrillard once called *that great whore on the other side of the desert,* as if femininity were nothing but a sordid lure, the mere sign of descent into the ineluctably artificial.

One night, back then, back when the fights erupted, a gang of four Argentinians appeared in the alley, a contingency from the gang Flores del Pampas, tough customers known for their sure-handed expertise and their merciless ferocity in the realm of knife fights. They rolled up in a blazing orange Firebird that snorted and screamed, all of them unbelievably young, not even men yet, all wearing the tallest pompadours any of the shirtless fighters had ever seen. Three of them got out of the car, which rumbled at their backs and blocked access to the street. They positioned themselves in a line and stood sentinel with their arms crossed and, it was reported, one hand inside their jackets. Two had hair as black as oil. One was a blonde with blue eyes and German blood. Don Aurelio's fighters and the few spectators who had wandered in from the streets and casinos searched the area around them, the dumpsters and trash cans and doorways, for any hiding places or blunt object that might have aided them in the coming onslaught. At some point, when the people in the alley were still frozen with alarm and indecision, a fourth shadow grew from the Firebird, folding forward through the passenger door and rising upright like an unforgiving god surveying a creation he despises. Which one of you is Frankie Reál? he said.

The scene afterward was bloodier than any horror movie set you could imagine, one of the first patrolmen to arrive later recalled. He described wide slicks of blood in which there floated fingers, pieces of scalp, ear, and chin, bits of material that could have been brain matter or ligament or the severed fragments of internal organs, it was impossible to tell. These weren't no paring knives, he said. He had indeed heard the rumors that the whole thing was staged, that it was in reality no bloodier than a horror movie set because indeed it really was a horror movie set, and all the blood and body parts spread across the alley behind the Golden Nugget were prosthetics, dyed corn syrup, and the police were too lazy or corrupt to even notice let alone test which parts allegedly belonged to which victims, or to investigate who the alleged victims even were. Those stories didn't come around until a few years after the fact, after the Flores refused to talk or skipped town and the whole thing went cold, the patrolman said.

Some other people, perhaps in response the horror movie explanation [though who could say which really came first], circulated a different rumor, stating the scene was indeed too real to imagine, that it was an authentic blood bath, and that someone had filmed the savagery with a handheld camera because the fight club liked to watch their rumbles and comment on them like baseball announcers. According to this rumor, the anonymous cameraperson had made a variation of the Zapruder film up to and including the dismemberment and shallow burial of Rosalita Sánchez, 16, said to have been seen on Frankie Reál's arm that evening, just outside the Nevada Test Site. Several frames of the burial sequence were said to have captured the distant lights of Las Vegas smeared vaguely across the eastern horizon, and the low rumblings of bomb detonations could be heard beneath the crazed laughing and coyote-like grunts of the young Flores del Pampas as they dug, though it could just as easily have been the sound of the idling Firebird.

But no, the horror movie theory, as opposed to the snuff film theory, accounted for these details. They were part of the terror. The Flores del Pampas were not a real gang, as their activities were not logged in any police file and their logo, a pair of roses whose thorny tendrils serpentined through the orifices of a bleached longhorn skull, was nowhere to be found in the youth gang task force's folder of insignias. They were an invention of the camera, purely fictional Cold War monsters poisoned by the downwind fallout of secret nuclear tests, and this spurred them to extreme violence, because they were angry at human imperialism and so no longer valued human life. It would be completely stupid to bury a body in that location, at any rate, the horror theory went, because it was certainly crawling with Army personnel, which meant it could only be a symbolic act to bury a murder victim there, and symbolic acts do not happen in real life.

Police and government corruption, the snuff film theory said. There was no official evidence of Flores del Pampas because the police accepted bribes from them and allowed them to terrorize Las Vegas with impunity, and the Army has made its living destroying the lives of black and brown people across the globe. Why should this be any different? The Flores del Pampas didn't value human life because they were simply monsters in their hearts, real ones, an American death squad, not because of radiation poisoning. And who directed this film, anyway, if it was the work of a deranged and disordered imagination? Who is responsible for it? None other than George A. Romero, a testament to his innovation as a filmmaker, a pioneering example of the handheld aesthetic that would not become common in film until camera phones. It was a terrible and inexplicably violent movie, make no mistake, which meant that Romero chose not to put his name on it or even distribute it—a rough draft, in essence—but one that did things with the lens no other filmmaker had ever yet conceived. Then where are the actors? Where are receipts? You want actors and receipts? Where's the body of Rosalita Sánchez? Have you dug her up and seen her for yourself? Where is she?

The patrolman, for his part, didn't know or care much about what to believe, a feeling he said was generally held throughout the LVMPD all the way up to the Chief of Police. If the film really exists, horror movie or not, I don't think it ever made its way to any evidence locker. When asked or prodded about the dismemberment and burial said to be a central moment in the footage, he said he didn't recall anyone named Rosa Sánchez ever being reported missing. But, he added, this didn't mean much.

[10]

The internet connection in Leo's hut is out this morning. Martha, his girlfriend in Poole, understands when he cannot immediately respond to her e-mails. He lives in exile on the Manpupuner Plateau in the Ural Mountains, a kilometer from the famed Seven Strong Man Rock Formations—one of the Seven Wonders of Russia that tourists frequently come to photograph—a two days' hike along the River Pechora to the nearest village. In his solitude, he has begun to write a novel about an American cowboy. Because the cowboy is an outlaw at heart, he gets the idea one day to approach a crew of Chinese railroad workers, pull his gun, and steal their horses. The team of soldiers hired to protect railroad property fires a volley of bullets as he rides away—a daring escape into the Utah desert. What's inventive, in Leo's opinion, is that the railroad crosses continents. His cowboy, raised to believe he is a Mormon, rides along the finished portion to San Francisco, up through British Columbia, the Yukon, and Alaska, then tramps over the mighty bridge spanning the Bering Strait into Russia [his horse is powerful and majestic, an immortal creature only he could tame], where the North American railroad connects with tributaries of the Trans-Siberian line. He follows the rails and ties across the steppe, eventually joining the main route and conforming to its meanders and curves until it branches off, leading him along a subsidiary line that connects to the famed Silk Road, opening the whole of Persia to his wanderings. He follows this well known route through Baghdad, the ruins of Antioch, and Istanbul [Leo, mindful of history, uses the old name Constantinople]. He envisions some event in the plot that will reveal the cowboy's true identity; he is not a Mormon, but a long-lost descendent of a royal lineage dating all the way back to Mesopotamia. The cowboy of course has many adventures along the way—gunfights, romances, captures and escapes. He is constantly disappearing into sunsets. At some point he teams up with a Mexican detective exiled in the Gobi Desert, and the two are either abducted by aliens and brought into the future or hallucinate while being tortured by a syndicate of Mongolian fur smugglers who fear law and justice. As always, the Cowboy and his sidekick escape, and in their victorious trot across the steppe they discuss the soul and fate and the destined place of the individual beneath the eternal stars. The Mexican detective disappears soon after their bold and heroic getaway. Leo does not remember why. The manuscript has piled up in his little cabin. He has written several million words in English, Russian, and Komi, the last having been the language his family spoke in his childhood home. To spare himself an unwieldy mess and, perhaps, to remember plot events written many months earlier, he has begun to pin pages to the wall. A tertiary benefit is that in doing so, he has also provided an abundance of fodder for bedtime stories to the boy he lives with. The boy is a story in himself. He never speaks. Leo has no idea of his origins, how old he is, or how long he plans to stay. He simply appeared like an empty bottle washed upon the shore. Leo had one day trekked back from the nearby aspen copse dragging a fox by its tail and carrying a bundle of traps over his shoulder. There the boy was, wandering the grounds around his hut in a pullover New York Knicks jacket and a yellow stocking cap. Leo is about to write the final sentence of a scene in which his cowboy outsmarts a contingent of brigands attempting to sell him into slavery when his phone pings. He opens the message from Martha. The subject line reads, *naughty boy*. He looks among sheets of paper out the window. The boy retreats into the sunset, heading toward the copse in the valley below. Leo opens a pornography streaming site on the web browser. Overhead, a tourist chopper clips past.

24

[11]

Media artist Grégory Chatonsky's *Telofossils* (2013), a collaboration with sculptor Dominique Sirois and sound artist Christophe Charles, pick up on this context of technologies, obsolescence, and fossils. The exhibition at the Museum of Contemporary Art in Taipei, Taiwan, focuses on the slow, poetic level of decay that characterizes technopolitical society and nature. The "future archaeologist" perspective that Chatonsky summons with immersive affective moods created in the exhibition's installations is akin to Manuel Delanda's figure of the future robot historian that gazes back at our current world emphasizing not the human agency of innovators, but the agency of the increasingly automated and intelligent machine (as part of the military constellation). The future archaeologist in Chatonsky's installations and immersive narrative is a displacement of the human from a temporal perspective [the future] and from the Outside [alien species]:

> *Telofossils* is a speculative fiction about this Earth without us. If another species arrives on Earth in thousands of years, what will it find? It will uncover from the ground billions of unknown objects with no apparent use, fossilized. It will certainly wonder why there are so many of them. A plastic bag can last hundreds of years when I only have 2,500 weeks left to live. This disproportion between the human life expectancy and the one of our technical artifacts gives a new dimension to our time. It will be a material trace for our memories. Making this absence and this disappearance visible is the goal of *Telofossils*, an impossible project.

Jussi Parikka, *A Geology of Media*

[12]

The Gold Rush is the mother ship in the Sea Queen Food Corporation's fleet of floating processors. For six weeks, it has been anchored in Norton Sound, a kilometer out from Nome in the Bering Sea. Henrik works as a processing technician, sorting fish by species, size, and condition, packaging and labeling product, inspecting it for quality, and tossing it into freezers. He possesses little to no engineering knowledge and so cannot tend to the ship's many engines and water pumps. Occasionally he will tighten a screw or a bolt that has come loose on a door or cabinet. His knowledge is primarily of the fish, picking the King from the Chum, Coho, and Sockeye, and of the ship's computer systems, for which he serves as the de facto network administrator, because the person officially hired in this capacity has grown suicidal and will not leave his quarters. Henrik picks, sorts, labels, freezes, and troubleshoots for twelve hours, then spends the next twelve barricaded in his cabin, where he builds websites, possibly without ever sleeping. He does not expect anyone to visit any of them. He seeks to contribute his share of useless content. His ideal website would be impossible to visit, whatever that could mean. Maybe someone has already made it, given that he can conceive of such a website but cannot visualize it or imagine how it might work. Maybe it steeps through the synthetic pores of broadband networks and screen. This way for ten weeks, a binary existence in which he is on then off the clock. He is a Norwegian by birth. The first website he ever made went live in 2001, shortly after 9/11. It was a very simple list of ideas for American television pilots that he named "The Discovery of the New World." The landing page presented a list of blue hyperlinks against a white background. Each link was numbered without a show title, *show 1 show 2 show 3*, all the way to *show 1492*. A user would click on a link, which routed them to a new page containing the description of the show. Most descriptions were basic treatments or synopses, although a handful contained spec scripts either in part, just a scene or two he had gotten bored with and abandoned, or in full, in both single- and triple-camera formats. One of these described a primetime hour-long drama in which actors play ordinary versions of themselves who had never become actors. It would be cast with washed-up TV stars from the seventies and eighties—Lee Majors the insurance claims adjustor, Valerie Harper the perfume counter clerk—so as to newly humanize their images and rejuvenate their appeal to mass audiences. Another link pulled up the description of a reality show in which several contestants per episode pitched television series to network and cable executives, which were either accepted for a price negotiated on the air or rejected with humiliating venom. He himself would deliver his pitch for this show to the decision makers at HBO, FOX, and the Big Three, who would either accept or reject him on live television. In other words, the pilot would be the pitch for the show itself. Under traditional broadcasting paradigms the show was a paradox, only possible to pitch if it had been green-lighted but impossible to green-light unless it was pitched. The pilot for this show could only exist on the plane of suicide bombings and guerilla warfare. For a while he imagined breaking the model of mass broadcasting as he sought to integrate himself in it—bursting into boardrooms with a small film crew and possibly a couple of rogue, underpaid production assistants who had access to their company's transmission infrastructures, until he realized he had no desire to actually make or even write for a television show. For a while, after seeing a video of a glacier the size of the World Trade Center's North Tower breaking off into the ocean, he curated a new website displaying a webcam feed of whatever body of water the *Gold Rush* happened to be anchored in. Occasionally a whale would appear, sometimes a leaping salmon, mostly the still, gray surface of the water silent beyond the steel gunwale. He still owns the domain though hasn't broadcast anything on it for months. Lately he has been working on a different site, one that requires him to steal fish. He loiters around the discard bin at the end of his shift and, as he is about to take off his hairnet and rubber gloves and return to his cabin, submerges his arms to the elbows, feeling for specimens with hard bulges in the gut. He gazes at the moon and stars as he strolls to his quarters, cradling the specimen like an infant. He plunks it down on the little wooden desk beside his bed and plunges a fillet knife into the belly. He whistles a tune as he works, something he dimly recalls from an earlier period in his life, or that he'd heard once in the distance. He opens the fish like a purse, turns it over, and dumps the foreign objects on the desk. Most of the time it's bottle caps, microplastics, fragments of credit cards, and pieces of netting, bits of debris that drift in ocean currents and accumulate at the interchanges, or that fishing crews discard at all hours of the day and night, every item making its way to the feeding grounds beneath the sea. The irony both fascinates and upsets him. For many of these fish, which often suffer from flavobacterium and other forms of virulence as signified by the skin lesions, eroded fins, and generalized necrosis degrading their bodies, the life-prolonging act of eating becomes a last meal, a feast of death. He arranges the plastics on a white surface lit by a dentist's lamp he had purchased in an online auction, placing them piece by piece in configurations he hopes reflect the muddled signals traveling along his synapses. He photographs these collages and uploads them to an online photo gallery. He does not exactly consider himself an artist or curator, but merely an activated person tending to the solitude of his situation. He has dreams of a movement to which no one but himself belongs.

[13]

At the Atlantic frontier one can study the germs of processes repeated at each successive frontier. We have the complex European life sharply precipitated by the wilderness into the simplicity of primitive conditions. The first frontier had to meet its Indian question, its question of the disposition of the public domain, of the means of intercourse with older settlements, of the extension of political organization, of religious and educational activity. And the settlement of these and similar questions for one frontier served as a guide for the next. The American student needs not to go to the "prim little townships of Sleswick" for illustrations of the law of continuity and development. For example, he may study the origin of our land policies in the colonial land policy; he may see how the system grew by adapting the statutes to the customs of the successive frontiers. He may see how the mining experience in the lead regions of Wisconsin, Illinois, and Iowa was applied to the mining laws of the Rockies, and how our Indian policy has been a series of experimentations on successive frontiers. Each tier of new States has found in the older ones material for its constitutions. Each frontier has made similar contributions to American character…

Frederick Jackson Turner, postulating American life as a
condition of virulence

[14]

A man owns a Flying-J Travel Center on a highway interchange
at the edge of the Omaha, Nebraska metropolitan area. It
faces north, looking out to County Road 31 and the off-
ramp connecting it to Interstate 80. The highway stretches to
the east and west along a series of replicating soybean fields,
vanishing at both horizons. In the distance, a water tower,
tractor dealership, and outlet mall are scattered among tree
belts planted to protect the topsoil. To the east is the city,
to the west more farmlands and Lincoln. He spends his days
in the office watching customers come and go on a 2x2 grid
of closed circuit television monitors stacked on his desk. He
imagines the sounds of their voices and the scents of their
perfumes, where they have come from and where their freshly
fueled vehicles will take them across the vast concrete network
of American roadways. They ride across the landscape on a
magic carpet of soybeans. He is summoned out of a reverie one
day by the teenaged cashier, who knocks on the office door and
tells him in a slightly frightened voice that a food shipment
has arrived, and its inventory is, in a word, unaccountable.
The truck driver refuses to leave until the store owner signs for
and receives this consignment of Sea Queen Alaskan Salmon,
twenty-six pallets each containing 2,250 10.5 oz. cans. The
driver has already unloaded half of them behind the store,
striding down the loading ramp with the laden pallet jack,
then back up for another load. He told me that he has to
keep moving, the clerk says. The driver halts his labor when
the owner comes out, curses the amount of time he has been
forced to wait, and shakes the work order at the owner's face,
pointing to the line where his signature is required. The owner
refuses to sign. The lingering images of his fantasies alternately
shred and cohere around the driver's face. He steps closer to

the angry driver, who has grown red around the temples and begun to throb in his entirety, and tells him and his cans to fuck off. In his dreams, every soybean is an individual voice within the vast organic chorus summoning minivans to this point of convergence. The driver shakes the work order. The owner mumbles something and throws his fist into the driver's ear. The man stumbles back with his hands and the work order pressed against his head. Fuck your shit, the driver says. The owner kicks him in the stomach. He drops to his knees and curses again. The teenage clerk watches in silence. The owner kicks the driver in the chest. He keeps kicking after the man has curled into a protective ball, aiming for the kidneys and ribs, kicking and kicking, bringing down his heel into the softest parts of the driver's torso, animated by the blood sputtering and seeping from the trembling mouth. Fuck your shit, the driver repeats despite the beating, as if these are the only words he knows, he keeps saying them until his voice is a fractured whisper or a wet cough, it might be the voice of the soybeans. Fuck your shit, the store owner himself silently repeats the phrase, he kicks until the flow of air ceases and the specter of families watching him from the gas pumps finally resolves. The driver is an ethnic Kurd. He had been a cab driver back in Syria. He fled Jarabulus a year before the Americans withdrew and allowed the Turks to cross the border and slaughter his family and friends. He made his way to Lebanon and embarked across the Aegean Sea on an inflatable raft with thirty other refugees. A number of them, the elderly and the small children, died of thirst and now rest under the water where surely the fish have picked them to the bone. He spent weeks in a camp in Greece before being resettled in Italy. He begged on the streets of Rome for an entire summer, sleeping on benches and stoops and with other Syrians in temporary camps on city squares. He asked Catholic pilgrims for money and food. He dreamed of being carried or teleported by God or magic or an intensity of his own will back to his home as he remembered it from childhood, all those years ago. He grew desperate, stealing from tourists and businesses. Near the end of his time in Italy he mugged a UNICEF worker at knifepoint, fleeing into the darkened alley. He walked across the border to Nice. He met a man there, an Iraqi, who offered to forge a passport in exchange for a large fee. He submerged himself in despair. One day an elderly woman who had never been outside the city crossed his path and took pity on him in spite of their religious differences. Perhaps she believed in charity or viewed him as an unhygienic urchin in need of a bath and several meals, or perhaps she hoped to convert him. Regardless of her motivation she invited him to her building and provided a secret bed for him in a dark corner of the boiler room. Two weeks later, feeling physically healthier but still unbearably depressed, he had accumulated enough money for the Iraqi and purchased a Tunisian passport. Americans can't tell the difference, the Iraqi said. They think I'm Greek or Egyptian. One man insisted I was a Spaniard. I think he was either a southern hick or college professor. They see the skin and the beard, or if you are a woman they look at your headscarf, and it's all the same to them. A lot won't like you. Most will pretend they do, they'll say nice things and put signs in their windows welcoming outsiders, but in their hearts they will despise you. They think it's all the same. He flew to Montreal. A month later he was in Pittsburgh waxing the floors of a famous gallery of dinosaur bones. As he pushed the buffing machine, inspecting his work every so often by gazing at his reflection in the enamel, he would ponder the Iraqi's warning. He was not sure how he felt about the United States. Most people walked past him without acknowledging his existence. Maybe they secretly hated him and wished for the extermination of his people, or maybe they genuinely did not notice that he existed, and it was their indifference to his presence that exterminated him. At the same time he recalled the American road movies he had enjoyed as a child, *Convoy* and *Easy Rider* and *Smokey and the Bandit* [he always thought Burt Reynolds could have passed as a Syrian], and as he fantasized about the television and VCR in his sister's bedroom, the smell of his mother's cooking wafting up the stairway, he got the idea to extend his journey perpetually, the big rig being in his mind the most luxurious form of itinerancy. All of this came out during the Flying-J owner's criminal trial. The beating, charged as attempted manslaughter, was designated as a hate crime, because every witness the police interviewed reported hearing the same racial slur burst like mortar fire from the owner's lips. During cross examination, the owner assumed the same deranged facial expression that emerged at the time of the attack, his eyes transforming into hot coals, his lips pulling back to reveal the murderous rictus of a wolf, and he began screaming nonsense at the stand about singing soybeans and how the sun used radiation to control his thoughts and tell him to automutilate. Then he bit into the flesh at the base of his index finger and bled all over himself and the witness stand and the bailiffs who rushed to constrain him. The judge called a mistrial and ordered the store owner unfit to participate in his own defense. He was remanded into medical custody until a new trial could be scheduled. His second trial did not have a jury. The judge found him guilty by reason of mental defect and ordered him to be securely hospitalized in the state mental institution. To this day, the store clerk says, he's up in the lunatic asylum north of Omaha, near the airport.

How long does he have to stay there? John Bearheart says.

I guess for his whole life.

What happened to the truck driver? Stan says.

I'm not sure. I think he was deported.

He was deported?

I think so.

That's insane.

So that's why you have all these cans of fish? John Bearheart says.

I wasn't working at the time, but that's what Amber told me. She's the clerk in the story.

The police didn't want it as evidence?

The clerk shrugs.

They both turn to look at the display, a mountainous formation touching the ceiling and nearly reaching the automatic doors. It emits a cultic vibration like a monument or shrine, intensifying the hum of the fluorescent lights. That's insane, too, he says.

[15]

Parallactic perspectives have introduced themselves into the new earth projects in a way that is physical and three-dimensional. This kind of convergence subverts gestalt surfaces and turns sites into vast illusions. The ground becomes a map.

Robert Smithson, "A Sedimentation of the Mind"

They have to double back thirty miles on Interstate 80 to reach the mental hospital. The GPS takes them through the downtown area, past the Union Pacific offices and one or two fountains shooting water from indeterminate forms of welded sheet metal that the city had probably commissioned from local artists, and through a labyrinth of residential streets, up and down double-lane boulevards separated by medians of trees and gardens. They turn a corner, and suddenly they are in front of the hospital. The building was erected in the early 20th century in the Collegiate Gothic style, popularized by the Cope and Stewardson architectural firm of Philadelphia. Of this genre of architecture, someone once said, *we find a new manifestation of one of the salient elements of medieval civilization. In our vanity we had forgotten it, and to that extent our civilization ceased to be Christian. The Philadelphia group has stood for and is standing for nationality, for ethnic continuity and for the impulses of Christian civilization* [*The Architectural Record*, vol. 16 no. 5, 1904]. Of course the building is an artifact of the American asylum movement. Stan feels as if he is staring into the annals of a mythical and absurd history. John Bearheart asks why on earth they'd put a place like this in the middle of a residential zone, then after a short pause declares that, judging by the preponderance of the craftsman style, the houses likely sprouted up around it after World War II. It must have been a major source of employment for returning soldiers, he says. Business must have been booming. They stand at the iron gate and gaze at the empty hospital grounds. The grass is long and gathers over the edges of the concrete and cobblestone walking paths. In the middle of the lawn, a dry fountain appears to have been decommissioned sometime long ago. The building itself might be abandoned. It stands six or seven stories high and stretches maybe a thousand feet in length. Neither man can tell exactly how far back it goes, or how much space separates it from the outbuildings visible in the distance. At the end of the block someone has fastened a sign to the fence, *No Vacancy*. John Bearheart rattles the gate and finds it is not locked. They pass through the hospital entrance, a beveled stone archway inscribed with a Latin phrase neither of them can decipher. They notice many things at once—foremost is the darkness emanating from the dead light fixtures, the overpowering scents of mildew and residual marijuana, water stains along the ceiling and walls, a mass of metal gurneys clogging the tiled foyer in front of the reception desk, littered with papers, pens, and open file folders the color of ripened wheat, and a discarded beer keg at the foot of the grand staircase, a small foamy puddle idling beside its rubber hose. Teenagers must party here, John Bearheart says. I guess so, Stan says. Maybe they inherit it if they spend the night. The gurneys seem like they have assembled to discuss the emptiness of the hospital and are trying to figure out what to do next. Stan feels three desires branching from a common ancestor. At once, he wants to proceed deep into the chamber of hallways, perhaps losing himself in some dark corner for the remainder of his life, never to be found by anyone, to melt where he is standing and become a puddle in which teenagers stomp the rubber soles of their sneakers on their way to and from the keg, and, last, probably best not to say. They think they hear a telephone ring somewhere and wonder who could possibly be calling, it must be a wrong number. They go back to the truck parked on the curb and ride Interstate 80 into the night, scanning the radio for songs and voices. It is too dark to see the buttes appear across the grasslands. At some point they're in Wyoming, high on a plateau, but they cannot tell the difference. John Bearheart smokes cigarette after cigarette.

He holds a can of salmon between his knees and picks out pieces with his fingers. Once or twice he expresses regret for wasting time at the hospital. What a bust, he says. Maybe it was the wrong building. What do you think? Stan watches the darkness fluctuate between surface and depth. Vague outlines might roll past on occasion. He tries to read, but he feels very tired. Maybe he flickers in and out of sleep. The same vibrating immobility disperses through him as when he finds himself in bed, aware that he is dreaming, only the dream belongs to someone else, someone from the past returning through his hazy wondering. Hell is a process.

[17]

As an artist I do not think about my work as related to
people first, although certainly the works I do are inclusive
of their audience. But they are actually and primarily an
exteriorization of my own interior reality. However, they are
also made so that people can be a part of them and become
more conscious of space, of their own visual perception and of
the order of the universe. But also, I think the work is about
'time'—a sense of time that is more universal. The works
really do function to keep time, to measure time. When I
build them, I think about human scale, and I think about
people standing in different places. In order to understand
and perceive my works one has to walk through them, in and
out of them, so that the works exist in durational time in that
respect. They are not just objects one sees in an instant, but
something one experiences in time.

Nancy Holt, Interview with Janet Saad-Cook

[18]

A filmmaker, Hideki, performs what he anticipates to be the final adjustment to the lens of his Canon Reflex Zoom 8. He has driven all the way out here in a rented 1964 ½ Mustang coupe [brand new, candy apple red] with Yasuko, his wife. She drinks a Coca-Cola in the passenger seat, watching him hunch forward with his eye in the view finder, twisting the aperture ring until the lens admits the optimal level of light. The sun is at its apex. The air temperature reaches nearly forty degrees Celsius. The ground, brittle and empty and astonishingly white, stinks of brine. Gazing toward the horizon, toward the distant mountains that edge this flat basin and seem to both levitate and melt into simmering mirages of water, she determines this is the point on Earth at which time and space collapse one into the other, confusing any possible logic to the ordering of each. She knows she will doubt its existence the moment they nose onto the highway and turn their backs. Only the sting of carbonized sugar water and the gleam of light on the Mustang's hood signal to her the potential for life. Lifting his fingers from the lens, Hideki smiles. His chin trembles. A tear drops to the salty crust and evaporates. *Pioneer*, he mumbles. *Go forth, young man...* Yasuko never fully learns of her husband's ambition for this project, his crusade, his righteous striving to accomplish on film what no one has been able achieve within the limitations of human sense and cognition, and thus an ambition to create an object that defies total consumption. Not on the drive to the motel nearer Salt Lake City. Not on their return journey across the salt flats, deserts, mountains, and coniferous forests culminating in their dinky studio apartment in San Francisco months later. Not in the years that pass. The camera stands on its tripod, an artifact recording the orbit of earth and stars, the slow entropy of geological time. That night, in the mental solitude that always culminates on the brink of sleep, Hideki imagines an infinite strip of film capable of capturing the totality of the planet's cosmological processes, a project that began before his birth, before animal birth as such, and that will continue beyond death. It is always in the middle of recording, always at the threshold of being remade. He rides this boundless loop through the night, toward a white hot beacon forever breaching the western sky.

[19]

The Great Pacific Garbage Patch is an unpopulated microkingdom divided into two accumulating continents, the "Eastern Garbage Patch" and the "Western Garbage Patch." Neither synthetic formation can be detected by imaging satellites, and they can rarely be seen by sailors, fishermen, or other humans who drift into their proximity. The masses are fundamentally moving and diaphanous, formed of loose aggregations of particles, wood pulp, and chemical sludge that are often microscopic and descend into the thermocline zone, beyond sight. Curation of the Great Pacific Garbage Patch is global, dispersed, and unmotivated. Plastics decompose in part by the application of light and air. The name of this process is photodegradation. The light can be steady and prolonged. It can be sudden and unimaginably severe.

[20]

She sees them emerge from the myrtle trees, two quivering
shadows, two leaning figures limping toward the vegetable
stands. She thinks one might be holding a bottle of gin.
By reflex, she inspects the rose bouquets to ensure they are
pleasantly arranged by quantity and color, the white icebergs
on one end of the counter, the pink moonstones on the other,
the classic reds between them, and that every bunch is easy
to grab, inspect, and purchase. There are many more figures
when she looks up, eight or nine zombies who moan and drag
themselves across the dirt and grass, all of them off-kilter and
on the verge of toppling. My God, someone yells. Several of
the ladies rush toward them, some others emit startled wails
or, as Silvia does, stand frozen in silence. For some reason,
she is smiling even though she might be going insane. Her
mouth is too parched to say anything. She might be made
of compacted dust, she might crumble and blow away if she
moves. She closes her eyes. A shadow falls across her.

The private eye never gave his full name. He refused the
beer she offered in the cantina after they had moved inside
from the rose garden. Eventually he asked if she knew what
xerophobia is. That's when people hate immigrants, she said.
They think foreigners take their jobs and carry diseases. Not
quite, he said. You're thinking of xenophobia. No, xerophobia
is different. I made that same mistake. He lit a cigar, puffing
until the end caught fire and moldered. Xerophobia, he said,
is the fear of dryness. A true xerophobe is terrified of a place
like this. He pursed his lips around the cigar, a cheap brand
emitting a fetid odor that instantly recalled to Silvia the garbage
heaps behind her childhood house. Imagine someone driving
for a long time, he said, maybe across the country, all the
way to California here, only to find out he has a pathological

aversion. It's too late by then. A guy in that situation might seek an outlet. She wiped her hands and forehead with a rag. The sunlight in the cantina had warmed and turned golden-orange at some point. The thin white curtains were saturated with dusk. Shadows spread across the flatness in the east. The first star appeared. So you're saying he's not from here? You're saying he's a lunatic who kills women and hacks them into pieces because he's afraid of the desert? No, the investigator said, holding his hands at chest level, as if to apologize for being too suggestive or to indicate he himself was unarmed. I'm not saying that at all. I'm not saying anything at this point. I just think there are some things that don't add up. After a while, he lit another cigar. Silvia again offered him a beer. He accepted this time. You know how many bodies are found in the desert every year? he said. The whole Southwest is a dumping ground. There are murders, of course, hundreds. Then there's the migrants who manage to wander across the border and die of dehydration. People set out barrels of water for them, but either ranchers or border agents tip them over or shoot holes in the sides. I guess xerophobia and xenophobia maybe aren't that unrelated. Maybe the two overlap in some cases. It could be what we're actually talking about here. It's not impossible that some new phobia exists at the border, some crazy association of what's dry and what's alien. Maybe it draws you in. Who can say? They talked about the missing woman long into the night. Men were always bringing her expensive gifts, Silvia said. Almost every day she hosted a client dressed from head to toe in black Gucci, turtlenecks and slim fitting pants, shining ankle boots with gold horse bits on the insteps, the word *kitten* painted on the high wooden heels. The same man every time? he asked. No, a different one, but they always dressed the same, as if they were part of a cult or it was their office uniform. She doesn't know if the woman ever slept with the men. In her opinion, they looked like homosexuals. Boxes came every day in the mail containing items from the most expensive fashion brands on the planet. She got this stuff for free. Silvia thinks the woman may have had a following on the internet. She might have been paid or gifted these things in order to generate a desire among her audience that could never be fulfilled. The woman wasn't subtle about it, either. She paraded everything around the farmhouse for all the ladies to see and marvel at. The investigator asked how the ladies accessed the internet in the house, whether they had their own laptops or tablets or if they used their phones, or if maybe they shared a desktop. He asked if he could take a look at the victim's laptop, assuming it was still in her room. Before he left [God only knew where this man lived], he asked Silvia how old she was and how long she had been working at the farm. She didn't know what to say. It seemed like he might be interested as a customer. Instead he adjusted the lapels on his raincoat and walked out the door with the missing woman's computer tucked beneath his arm. She went upstairs, wiped tears from her eyes and cheeks, and reapplied her eyeshadow for Rafael, breathing deeply, listening to the investigator's car whinny and sputter until finally the engine turned and he cruised away.

The people scraping across the lawn stink of gasoline and sweat. They are alive. Three of them lie on their backs in the middle of a patch of dirt while the ladies ask them questions, stroke their foreheads, and call for shade. The others mill around, two of them leaning against the side of the house, attempting to catch their breath. The remaining three simply appear stunned, gazing at the sky. They are all vacationers from Osaka. Every one of them is over sixty-five years of age. Seven speak fluent English and explain that their tour bus crashed on a sharp curve at the end of the drive. They were on their way to Joshua Tree, after which they were supposed to go to the Carlsbad Caverns, then the Trinity Test Site at Jornada del Muerto, then Los Alamos, and finally Fort Sumner to see where Pat Garrett shot Billy the Kid. Silvia cannot bring herself to go look at the crash or help the victims who are trapped in the wreckage or otherwise unable to walk. She watches what could be a wisp of smoke spread and disappear above the treetops. Shortly after the final ambulance departs for San Bernardino, a TV crew arrives. They interview the triaged victims and several Black Rose residents. The evening report explained that the driver, 21, was a local college student who did not possess the proper license or experience to operate a charter bus. He was the son of the touring company's owner. He told police that he hated his job and that he got high on mushrooms an hour before departure. He sped as fast as he reasonably could in order to minimize the duration of the trip. He thought he saw a rift in the earth filled with millions of hybrid coyote-men and swerved to avoid a fall into the underworld, because he was beguiled by the delusion that driving into the gulf, which appeared thousands of miles wide and infinitely deep, would trigger a shock wave strong enough to instantly end the totality of life on the planet. There were deaths and dismemberments [the report did not mention the latter]. The exact number, as of the time of the report, could not be determined, and the accident did not appear to be related to the missing woman, of whom there were no major updates to report other than the one about her clothing, as police had now confirmed that she had last been seen wearing a short kaftan dress and matelassé espadrilles from Gucci's new summer collection. Silvia watched it on TV with the other ladies. They passed glasses of beer around the living room and commented on the broadcast as if they were critics or baseball announcers. When the news broke for commercial,

Silvia went to the bathroom. As she urinated, she discovered the feeling that she had seen all of this in a different life from a different perspective, only what she had witnessed was not a bus crash or a summative narration of its causes and effects, and the different viewpoint from which she saw this other thing somehow overlapped with the life she now lived on a day to day basis, but without ever quite merging with it—a path that was contiguous but not continuous with the one she traveled every day, so to speak, like a dream that lingers in the brain for the first few moments after waking, then disappears completely from memory. Here was a linkage, a blurry edge, that did not reveal itself in full. She returned to the living room and sipped another beer. Her image appeared on the screen. A branded chyron indicated her name and status as witness. As a viewer, she both did and did not recognize herself explaining the horror of that afternoon. There was Silvia up there on the screen, good old Silvia trembling and speaking softly into a microphone from the distant past, uttering words she does not remember saying. That's when I finally understood that I had to get out of there, she says. I would die if I stayed. I might not even be alive now. I had to get moving and never stop. So I came to San Francisco. Here I am, Rafael. What's new? Is everything okay?

[21]

A few cars come and go at the salt flats rest terminal, even in the middle of the night. Voyagers, one may assume, passing from place to place. The Canon Reflex Zoom 8 stands in the middle of the basin, fixed on the earth and sky. The mountains recede into the night, marked only by the absence of stars across their shadowy fissures. Beyond them, the lens captures the slow turn of the horizon in relation to the ancient Pleiades, Aldebaran [the red giant] blazing in the eye of Taurus. Roving constellations, moonlight on the parched terrain, pipes linking rest stop urinals to the municipal sewer system of West Wendover, Nevada, highway silent as time, the camera itself, its operations and its ultimate purpose.

[22]

The United Micro Kingdoms (UmK) is divided into four super-shires inhabited by Digitarians, Bioliberals, Anarcho-evolutionists and Communo-nuclearists. Each county is an experimental zone, free to develop its own form of governance, economy and lifestyle. These include neoliberalism and digital technology, social democracy and biotechnology, anarchy and self-experimentation and communism and nuclear energy. The UmK is a deregulated laboratory for competing social, ideological, technological and economic models.

United Microkingdoms: A Design Fiction
[http://unitedmicrokingdoms.org/]

[23]

Pancho and Itsumi, who he insists on calling Lefty, nose onto the Central Freeway in San Francisco's Mission District, ride the long curve through fields of warehouses, machine shops, storage units, and refurbished luxury apartments, and head toward the Bonneville Salt Flats 700 miles east. Pancho rides shotgun with a bare foot hanging out the window. Long ago, before he can remember, he gave up wearing shoes.

[24]

She may carry a knife or razor—often for self-protection against her customers. A prostitute is not in a position to call the police if her customer should assault her "just for kicks" or to get his money back.

Jerome H. Skolnick, *Justice Without Trial*

[25]

It was the disappearances in the north and especially in Nogales and Cuidad Juárez that drew him to Mexico, the disappearances and a book he had recently read called *2666*. He drove his piece of shit car up and down the desert highways, through Sonora, Chihuahua, Durango, Zacatecas [where for some reason he knew John Wayne had filmed *Big Jake* in the early 70's], San Luis Potosi, and Veracruz, then back again several days or weeks later, sometimes branching into Coahuila or Nuevo León or Sinaloa, passively imagining certain scenes and characters he remembered from Bolaño's tome as the blunt desolation of the landscapes passed in front of him, often nothing but dust and scrub and distant hills, excepting the beaches on the coasts or the Occidental or Oriental spans of the Sierra Madre or the grassy plains of the Mexican Altiplano, which lifted him somewhat from his dreamlike memories and caused him to finally take notice of his surroundings. Every so often he would realize that he was dreaming of Bolaño's mysterious narrator or the corrupt or disenchanted Mexican detectives tasked over many years with finding a city's worth of missing women and girls, detectives who themselves appeared and disappeared from the text like ghosts or the corpses they were called to investigate. The realization that he was dreaming only intensified his desire to return to the enchanted state from which he had awakened. He would light a cigar, feeling irritable, and turn the dial on the radio in search of static, which he found served as effective white noise in his pursuit of waking sleep. At some point the reveries would reassemble. His sense of existence would become as flat and blank as the red wastes sprawling on all sides from the highway.

He found a place to stay on the Baja California side of Tecate, a mirror zone of factories, breweries, and highways cutting through the sprawling neighborhoods and slums that ended on one side in open desert and in the tall border fence and port of entry on the other, which accessed Tecate, California, USA. For the first few nights he either parked his car in abandoned lots and slept in the front seat, or else he went from bar to bar and drank until the sun came up and the coffee shops and cafés were open. On the last of these first nights, he found himself in a pool hall with a small dance club in the basement. He felt as if he was keying in on something, as if he was a high-tech pharmacological product engineered to destroy some novel pathogen. He had questions to ask, but he did not know what they were or to whom he should direct them. The bar was full of men in blue jeans and sweaty shirts, men who worked in the brewery or maquiladoras or some nearby ranches. He thought maybe it was a gay bar, which he didn't mind. He ordered three fingers of whiskey and waited. The few women in the place were either employees or very young, the latter in line for admittance to the dance floor downstairs. The purple and blue and red lights brought out features of their ensembles that would never be visible in the light of day. The colors seemed to slow and aggrandize the ordinary movements of their bodies—drawing a tendril of hair behind an ear, bending and straightening legs eager to let loose, pulling a cell phone from a tiny purse that was normally white or cream colored but in this realm alternated orange and red—he felt as if he was looking at the models from which all humans originated, or the android-like refractions of a never-ending music video. They wore varieties of clubbing outfits, tight sequined dresses that covered maybe half of their thighs, tall shoes, glittery makeup dusting their eyes, cheeks, and collarbones. They milled in groups of three or four, some of them there with their boyfriends, who in comparison were dressed to clean toilets. He figured they were all factory or sex workers or maybe in a couple of cases both. What could he say upon approaching them other than describing his fatalistic sense that the future has already stamped itself on the present? He drank some more, thinking of the Bolaño book and the news stories about bodies in the desert that he had looked up after he had finished the novel, as if to relive the adventure of the fiction and the more notable moments of his former life that the book had caused him to remember. All of it—the ink, microfilms, and websites—constituted some perverse witchcraft or a magical architecture that extended both his reading and his memory beyond page and neuron, reanimating them as active and objective forces in the world. Then without trying too hard he thought back to some of the cases he had variously solved and fucked up years ago for the LAPD. He had owned only two cars in his life: the one he drove as a homicide detective, and the one he drove in private practice. He had a wife for a while.

He asked the bartender's name after ordering his third or fourth whiskey. Miguel, the bartender said. He was much shorter than the men playing pool and dressed like a successful club owner or the president's son. The lighting made it hard to say exactly what color his suit was. The inspector guessed navy blue or maybe some mellow shade of purple. He couldn't see the shoes. Maybe something without laces, a snakeskin or white leather loafer with a gold horsebit below the tongue. The guy wasn't wearing a tie, only a white shirt unbuttoned at the top with a tall and very stiff collar. A bartender in a suit, he thought. He wondered how Miguel managed to keep himself immaculate despite pouring drinks, spinning bottles, and wiping glasses. There wasn't so much as a droplet of liquor anywhere on him, not even his shirt. Miguel wiped a portion of the bar and leaned an elbow against it, as if prompting the inspector to ask more questions. A group of loud American tourists in cowboy hats and sombreros came in as he was thinking of something to say. They were all men, college aged, probably down from San Diego. They went straight for the jukebox, yipping and shooting at each other with toy pistols, and queued up a long sequence of Johnny Cash songs. The pool players stood upright for a moment before returning to their games. Miguel muttered something that the investigator couldn't understand. He wasn't sure if it was Spanish or English or one of the local Indian languages. He ordered a Tecate to go with his whiskey. Can or draft? Miguel said. Whichever is bigger, he said. He asked if Miguel had ever heard of the desaparecidos.

Nothing in the papers?

Who reads the papers?

Nothing online?

I only read the sports columns, Miguel said.

The line for the dance floor had grown at some point. It went out the door, and when the investigator got outside he saw that it wrapped around the block. He sat in his car and watched them, all these women and girls that he imagined weren't any older than fifteen or sixteen, not old enough to vote or legally purchase liquor but that probably worked in the smokestacks along the border, a small country of children waiting to descend a set of stairs to a basement that was far too small to hold them all at once. He imagined the soil beneath each set of feet, the dust that would remain after they stepped forward, through the door. He dreamed of this empty earth. A borderless, ransacked immensity cleared of all life and the basic potential to sustain it. Time was marked by an occasional face vaguely taking shape in the dirt. He could not tell if it was the same face or a new one each time. Inevitably it blew away. At some point the sun came up, a blood-red fireball blazing in the east.

[26]

I started *Sun Tunnels* in 1973. It was from being in the desert
that I really started to perceive the sun. Here in the city I am
aware of it—my windows overlook the sunset—but nothing
like in the desert where one is overwhelmed by the sun.
After the idea for *Sun Tunnels* evolved out of my being in the
western desert, I looked all around for land to buy in order
to make it. I found the right site in the Great Basin Desert in
northwestern Utah. It is a very desolate area, but it is totally
accessible, and it can be easily visited, making *Sun Tunnels*
more accessible really than art in museums. The 'best' thing
that can happen to a traditional sculpture is that it is bought
by a museum. It is then usually put into storage and not even
the artist can get to see the piece. A work like *Sun Tunnels* is
always accessible—it's as accessible as the Grand Canyon. And
we do have a tradition of going around in cars and looking at
remote places. Eventually, as many people will see *Sun Tunnels*
as would see many works in a city—in a museum anyway.

Nancy Holt, JS-C Interview

[27]

The writer Italo Calvino posited the existence of magical objects, such as a bone or an automobile. Once it enters a story, the bone or car or other magical thing automatically engages a special form of sorcery enabling it to draw the entire world toward itself, it is a charged node conjuring a network of relations. Calvino also expressed a sense that the whole world was slowly petrifying and turning to stone. He asked what would happen if it were to stop turning.

[28]

The investigator, who calls himself Romano, woke up staring at imprints of the sun floating on his retinas, thinking of spots revealed by black lights at real or imagined crime scenes—floor tiles, carpets, walls, curtains, hotel bedspreads… At the scene of any crime, the detective becomes a minor historian specializing in a hyperlocal data field. This person thinks of ordinary objects and the relations between them, some emphasized over others and in different combinations, and in doing so glimpses the outer edge of a vast and terrible secret.

He drove his piece of shit car along a series of highways and interchanges, often forgetting where he was and where he might be going. He stopped for an hour or an afternoon in Caborca without noticing any of the colonial missions or local storefronts or franchises of transnational chains. The world began in his windshield and terminated at the horizon. A group of dirt bike racers overtook the cantina where he ate lunch and drank. They bought him beer after beer, not any brand he had heard of, possibly not any brand at all, maybe a home brew kept in plastic buckets beneath the counter. The youngest of the racers, an Anglo teenager from Montana, let him ride his bike in the dirt behind the bar. He revved the engine and kicked up a plume of red dust and tipped over. They vomited together behind a pig trough somewhere in the countryside, where an old Indian woman watched them from behind a fire pit with no obvious expression on her face. He noticed stars in the east and turned toward Hermosillo. The desert air is an opacity revealing nothing of itself. He thought entirely with his hands and feet. The only thing to do was go deeper into it.

[29]

A natural pigment-based ephemeral work created on a dry
lake bed in the Mojave Desert, *Rock and Pigment Installation*,
reflected the sky, with rocks placed in alignment to the stars
overhead.

Lita Albuquerque, description for *Rock and Pigment Installation
Mojave Desert, CA 1978* [litaalbuquerque.com/1978/10]

[30]

He drove for a week or more, possibly in circles, filling his piece of shit car at service stations built in the middle of the desert, miles and miles from anything. At some moments he thought the landscape was really the dusty void he had seen in his dream outside the club in Tecate, that all the children in the world had descended an invisible staircase to an inaccessible dance club that didn't actually exist. He soon realized how drunk he always was, how drunk and how tired, and that he was constantly snapping awake. He filled his car with gas at these lonely stations, which may have been their own country because they all looked alike and seemed to be staffed by the same teenage clerk who was stoned or maybe possessed with a sadness so deep and profound that it wasn't actually sadness, but a grimy and unbearably dense sensation only the clerk could feel and that he expressed in his ballad-like recitations of gas charges and sales tax, and purchased himself a fresh case of Tecate that he consumed one by one as his foot pressed on the gas pedal. He could not say how fast he drove or whether he had hit and killed anything attempting to cross the highway or whether any police had attempted to pull him over. He simply arrived in Xalapa as if stepping through a doorway—he was not there, and then he was. He leaned against the hood of his car, lit a cigar, and folded his arms, watching a crew of half a dozen city workers dig a trench in the grass of Parque Juárez across the street. They worked among hedges and flowers, beds of different varieties of roses, under the conjoined shadow of several trees. The shadow gradually broke apart in many quivering fragments that slimmed and shortened to nothing. By then, the workers had stuck their shovels in the ground, circled under the shade of a single araucaria tree, and pulled sandwiches and water bottles from their lunch coolers. A trio of jazz musicians, a trombonist and a snare drummer and standing bass player, had assembled on the wide courtyard between shady lawns and was playing a fast-paced number, maybe a variation of Frank Rosolino or Roy Haynes, something improvised and on the verge of breaking loose. Romano drove through the city center, looking for a place to eat and maybe drink a cold beer or two. He passed several points of interest, the Carlos Fuentes Library and an art gallery devoted mostly to Diego Rivera's works, a couple of municipal buildings that struck him as the stuff of movie sets or the old European world—stacks of columns and porticos and arched windows and balconies girded by iron rails, several of which displayed mannequins in what he took to be Revolution-era dress, an impression that derived mainly from the glut of Westerns he had consumed as a kid. He thought maybe he had wandered into some local celebration. People were smiling and seemed at the very most only passively aware of their surroundings. Most pushed strollers or carried shopping bags and wore expensive clothing. They gazed into store windows, strolled in and out of shops holding the hands of their loved ones, some also clutching paper Starbucks cups with sleeves around them to protect them from the machine-calibrated heat of their coffee drinks. It occurred to him that despite his intentions, which he did not understand and may have been imaginary or an abyss into which the rest of his psychology was on the brink of falling, he was a tourist. He eventually found a café near the stadium, a little ways out from the city center. He sat at a plastic table with a floral vinyl covering. The chair was also plastic and displayed the café's logo on the backrest, the name of which he cannot make out when he tries to remember. He ate a dish of crispy plantains and french fries with a cut of grilled pork and a salad of lettuce and pickled carrots. He drank three cold pints of Tecate. The person waiting on him was very young, a girl of maybe fourteen or even thirteen. She wore a black apron and a bright blue t-shirt and Spandex athletic pants, smiling amicably as he stumbled through his order and when she brought him his food and beer several minutes later. He could hear her talking to someone and laughing in the kitchen as he ate. For the duration of his meal, he was the only person in the room. His eye continually drew away from the baseball game playing on a little flat screen TV in the corner to a framed mirror on the wall. He realized after staring for a minute or two that it was not really a mirror, but a painting, and that it photorealistically displayed what a person sitting in his chair would see if it were to actually be a reflective pane of glass—the triangular segment of turquoise and yellow floor tiles, the green baseboard running diagonally across the canvas, the yellow wall and the corner of a laminated menu hanging from it. Perfect details. Perfect lines. Perfect color and shading that miraculously fused with the time of day. Perhaps more perfect than the place itself. Two police officers came in as he was finishing his last beer. They of course spoke to each other in Spanish. The only words he could make out, which upon hearing them in the little café he suddenly and shamefully recalled having spoken himself in every town where he had stopped, were chica and puta. He lit a cigar as he ambled toward the door. The policemen went silent and watched him pass, as if they were guarding something sacred or volatile and extremely dangerous. He found it strange that one of them was a redhead with green eyes and freckles and a thick and rusty mustache that reminded him of Wyatt Earp's. He slept in his car in the stadium parking lot. The next morning he drove around the suburbs and watched a group of children play a pickup game of baseball in a vacant lot. Besides the waitress, he could not remember the last person he actually spoke to. A couple days later he was back in Tecate.

[31]

During the past three centuries the spread of the English-speaking peoples over the world's waste spaces has been not only the most striking feature in the world's history, but also the event of all others most far-reaching in its effects and its importance. The tongue which Bacon feared to use in his writings, lest they should remain forever unknown to all but the inhabitants of a relatively unimportant insular kingdom, is now the speech of two continents. After the great Teutonic wanderings were over, there came a long lull, until, with the discovery of America, a new period of even vaster race expansion began. There have been many other races that at one time or another had their great periods of race expansion—as distinguished from mere conquest,—but there has never been another whose expansion has been either so broad or so rapid as the Englishmen's. The English race has a perfectly continuous history.

Teddy Roosevelt, *The Winning of the West: From the Alleghenies to the Mississippi*

[32]

Digitarians depend on digital technology and all its implicit totalitarianism—tagging, metrics, total surveillance, tracking, data logging and 100% transparency. Their society is organised entirely by market forces; citizen and consumer are the same. For them, nature is there to be used up as necessary. They are governed by technocrats, or algorithms—no one is entirely sure, or even cares—as long as everything runs smoothly and people are presented with choices, even if illusionary. It is the most dystopian, yet familiar of all the micro kingdoms.

[http://unitedmicrokingdoms.org/digitarians/]

[33]

Pancho and Itsumi, who he insists on calling Lefty, nose onto the Central Freeway in San Francisco's Mission District, ride the long curve through fields of warehouses, machine shops, storage units, and refurbished luxury apartments, and head toward the Bonneville Salt Flats 700 miles east. Pancho rides shotgun with a bare foot hanging out the window. Long ago, before he can remember, he gave up wearing shoes…

He circled the streets of Tecate well into the night, searching for the pool hall with the dance club in the basement. He drove up and down Federal Highway 2, through the outskirts, into the desert, and back. He could not find it. He bought food at a stand that sold chili and hamburgers. He drove through the industrial parks strung along the border that emitted light and steam every hour of the day, then he cut south through a middle-class neighborhood of two-story homes that reminded him of the suburbs of L.A. and Alameda County. Maybe because he was exhausted or because his hands were beginning to shake he settled on a dingy little place off the main street, a few blocks from the brewery. The bar was staffed by a skinny and miserable looking old man who nodded and jabbered as Romano placed his order. Possibly the man didn't even work there, the place might not have been officially open. The old man, dressed in a San Diego Chargers t-shirt and jogging pants and rubber sandals, might have wandered in days ago and helped himself to the tap. Romano ordered some whiskey but got a tall can of beer instead. He smoked cigar after cigar. For hours he and the old man were the only people in the room. It was dark. They did not talk. Every so often a set of headlights would pass and cast their light through the narrow and dusty window in the door. A radio behind the bar was tuned to a local station playing nothing but Norteño polkas. The old man stood next to it with his hands in his pockets, staring vaguely at the ceiling, where his gaze fanned out and vanished. Romano assumed he would spend the night in his car again or maybe skip sleeping and cross into the U.S. and get back to L.A. before sunrise. He could not say why, but the idea of going home seemed unbearable, like he had swallowed a spoonful of something that turned his guts into stone. He lit another cigar, ordered another whiskey, and received another beer. The discrepancy made him smile. He wanted to see how far he could take it. He slugged the can and asked for a gin martini, then a plate of cappelletti, then a brand new Ferrari. The old man, a zombie or a corpse raised by the necromancy of ordering patrons, bent forward and pulled a fresh can of beer from the little fridge under the bar every time. Romano flicked the ashes from his cigar. He wondered if he had actually wrecked his car and died. All the children in the world might have vanished. Another man entered shortly after the window had begun to wake and redden, tossing the door open and striding through the sunrise filling the threshold. He was tall and thick, around six-foot-three and maybe two hundred and forty pounds, he nodded at Romano and addressed the old man in English and by name. Two Bloody Marys, Paco, for me and my friend here, he said, plunking down next to the investigator and giving him a wink. Romano inhaled deeply and twisted on the stool first one way and then the other, stretching all the small muscles from his ass to his shoulders. I must have dozed off, he said. And a coffee, too, Paco. Actually, make that two. Two Bloody Marys and two coffees. The hottest and freshest you got. The drinks appeared in front of them as if a sorcerer had said the magic words. They drank without speaking very much, briefly exchanging names and making intermittent comments on the smell of the brewery, which never ceased and dominated this part of the city. After the coffees and Bloody Marys they switched to beer, the same cans Romano had been slugging all night. Eventually it came out that the big man, whose name was Aurelio, was actually Aurelio Saavedra, and he was the fourth outfielder for the 1973 World Series Champion Oakland Athletics.

You don't seem old enough, Romano said.

It's the tomato juice, Saavedra said.

A while later they decided to find a spot for breakfast, since Paco didn't cook. The bar looked different in the daylight, a small square building on the corner rather than the shadowy niche Romano thought he had stepped into. He studied the iron bars on the windows and door and the cracks in the plaster siding. There was no sign on the front or mounted on a pole in the cement. Maybe it didn't have a name. A few cars were parked up and down the curb among palm trees and marigold bushes. The street was wet from an overnight rain shower and led to the neighborhoods he had driven through the night before in one direction and the downtown area in the other. He fanned himself with the lapels of his raincoat and asked what time it was. Saavedra checked his iPhone and said it was 9:30. Unbelievable, Romano said. It must be ninety degrees already. How does that happen after a rainstorm? He felt the pockets in his pants and jacket. I don't remember where I parked, he said. Fuck me. Saavedra said it wasn't a problem, he knew a place close by. The big man led him down the street, around a corner, through an alley, under a bridge, and around another corner to a coffee shop several blocks away. They chose to sit at a wrought iron table on the sidewalk in the shade of a palm tree. Romano found the café pleasant. The little terrace was decorated with a profusion of flowers and bushes. He couldn't name most of them except for the roses. Nonetheless he closed his eyes and tried to appreciate the mingling perfumes, which vaguely reminded him of something and worked somewhat to mask the odor of the brewery. It wasn't until his eyes were closed that he realized how dry they were and how badly they stung. Neither man talked about anything until the waitress brought their food and coffee, at which point Saavedra started in on a couple stories about Sal Bando's cock and some prank he claimed Rollie Fingers once pulled on a busboy in Chicago.

The café didn't serve liquor, so they went to another place around the corner after they finished their meal. After two or three whiskeys, Saavedra volunteered that he didn't stay in Tecate all the time. He had a place in the East Bay where he went for a couple of months every year, sometimes six or eight or all twelve in the calendar, when the mash started to smell like death, which could not be predicted and had nothing to do with the weather. Romano asked how long he'd been in Mexico. I remember you on that Oakland team. I grew up in Hayward, so I remember watching you on the tube and hearing your name now and then on the radio broadcasts. We'd make it down to the Coliseum once or twice a year. I might have seen you play. The big man grinned and signaled the bartender for another round. I bounced around until seventy-five or seventy-six, he said. It's hard to remember exactly. Carter was president, I know that. I signed with the White Sox and then the Rangers, or the Rangers and then the White Sox, and spent a couple years on one of their Triple-A teams, or Double-A, I don't fucking remember. That life seems like it never really happened. They got a team here. My family was here. After a few more rounds, as the sun passed its apex and began its descent toward the west, the investigator told him about Bolaño's book and how the author died from cirrhosis before it was published. He spoke of the narcos and news reports and the legions of missing girls and the secret reality of unmarked graveyards scattered across the deserts all around North and South America and the fields of Europe and every other populated continent. I knew you were law enforcement, Saavedra said. I took one look at you and I knew you were a cop. You must be after someone. That's the funny part of it, Romano said. He turned on his stool and gazed out the window, leaning his back against the bar with his elbows resting on it. Foot traffic had picked up as they drank. People were out shopping, walking to and from their shifts at the brewery and boutiques and offices and cafés and factories. Later, Saavedra brought Romano to a building around the corner where he rented a room. At most it was maybe two hundred square feet, a brick and plaster hovel with a futon in one corner and a desk holding a computer and small television in another. Saavedra had torn pictures of ball players from different issues of *Sports Illustrated* and printed some from the internet and pinned them to the walls along with one of Clint Eastwood as Josey Wales and another of Kris Kristofferson. None of the photographed ball players were Saavedra himself, from what Romano could tell. On the far wall, difficult to see in the play of shadows and light, was a kitchenette—a hotplate, a frying pan hanging on a hook beside the window, a sink, a couple cabinets and drawers, and a miniature refrigerator. There was a toilet and shower on the floor upstairs and also one of each on the ground floor near the lobby, Saavedra informed him. The place was sparse but lived in. This is where I stay when I'm downtown, he said, which is usually a couple nights a week. There are some women on the outskirts and in Tijuana who let me rotate between them. I'll make you a key. You can stay here as often as you want. I'll sleep on the floor or at one of my friends' places. I don't give a shit. You're a good guy. He proceeded deep into the room and opened a drawer in the kitchenette and showed Romano the Desert Eagle .44 Magnum he kept beside some potholders and a wooden spoon and a set of tongs and what was either a polished bolt or a World Series ring. They took turns holding the firearm and admiring its heft before Saavedra put it back and they left to fetch the investigator's car. One day Romano watched a CNN segment about a mass grave that had been discovered in the desert in Veracruz, a growing pit that contained the remains of at least 250 men, women, and children kidnapped by the drug cartels since the government declared war on organized crime in 2006. It was a dumping ground, apparently, a horrible abyss that grew and deepened with every passing year. He wrote down all of the important details from the CNN report, then met Saavedra at the bar around the corner where they had drunk after their seminal breakfast. The bar was named Rosa's Cantina, probably to remind the Americans who came down on the weekends of the sticky-sweet cowboy ballads of Marty Robbins, or if they had never heard a Marty Robbins song—if they were young or had forgotten the past and therefore had no idea who Marty Robbins was—it would probably at the very least make them think of the Old West. They drank all day and went to a dance club after the sun went down. Saavedra left around midnight with a woman one-third his age. Romano drank gin until the place closed at six in the morning. A few days later he watched a Telemundo report in the apartment with Saavedra, who translated. The field reporter described a brothel that doubled as an organic vegetable farm on the outskirts of Los Angeles, in San Bernardino. He described the woman who had gone missing, the number of kidnappings in the Mojave region every year, those related to the narcos and those that resulted from other gang activities and domestic disputes and chance occurrences and those related to coyotes and polleros smuggling people across the border, all part of the legacy of bodies that returned in the receding sands. He mentioned a bright red vintage Mustang, a young man who wore the desert on his clothes. A youth, he said, who the people have informally dubbed Billy the Kid.

[35]

American president Harry S. Truman said the atomic bombs dropped on Hiroshima and Nagasaki on 6 August and 9 August 1945 proceeded from *harnessing the basic power of the universe*. It was *the force from which the sun draws its power* that *had been loosed against those who brought war to the Far East*. Truman is not conventionally known as a worshipper of the sun.

[36]

The Communo-nuclearist society is a no-growth, limited population experiment. Using nuclear power to deliver near limitless energy, the state provides everything needed for their continued survival. Although they are energy rich it comes at a price—no one wants to live near them. Under constant threat of attack or accident, they live on a continually moving, 3 kilometre, nuclear-powered mobile landscape. Consequently, they are organised as a highly disciplined mobile micro-state. Fully centralised, everything is planned and regulated. They are voluntary prisoners of pleasure, free from the pressures of daily survival, communists sharing in luxury not poverty. Like a popular night club there is a one-out one-in policy, but for life.

[http://unitedmicrokingdoms.org/communo-nuclearists/]

The fish collages have gone viral. A rapper famous for his mental illness posted some of them to his Instagram account. His wife, a reality TV star whose father was one of the shadow lawyers who had helped prosecute Saddam Hussein [he was also rumored to have recorded and disseminated the cell phone video, for all intents and purposes a snuff film, of the Iraqi dictator's inglorious hanging], had created a brand for her eponymous clothing empire in which mass produced cotton t-shirts and sweatshirts are printed with images of Henrik's work. The clothes are in rapid production now, as Henrik scrolls the web browser—a growing fleet of beautiful people wear them and pose for photographs in the Southern California sun and post these images to their own accounts for pay. Some venues report the rapper and reality TV star have re-named their three year old daughter TeloKingHenrik, a decision that has raised questions among the paparazzi and gossip columnists in part for its suggestion of lunacy and in part for the mystery of its first and third and components, *Telo* & *Henrik*, which strike the eye as odd and out of place and basically arbitrary. The rapper and his fashionista wife apparently like to play coy or crazy in their interviews. The name is the fulfillment of a demand made by Gabriel, a mashup of both spouses' middle names, a linguistic representation of their house, which is made of three loosely related but aesthetically distinct wings, or an honorific indicating the child's inborn regality, for she was prophesied in a dream and born with a caul. On and on.

Sorting fish one night, Henrik recalls thinking of impossible websites and suspects that he finally understands what he meant, and that they are not impossible, but in fact they are everywhere and color one's awareness of space and movement, and so constitute an ontology—a digital consciousness, or a web-based understanding of the world. The span of the little table where he makes his collages turns out to be a fundamentally creative space, a virtual dimension of pure potential that bleeds into the rest of the cabin, the *Gold Rush*, the Bering Sea, the ocean as a whole, the landmasses drifting tectonically like time across it.

He posts to certain image boards that he himself is the one responsible for the production of the fish collages, which he calls *telofossils* after coming across the phrase somewhere, though he has long forgotten the actual source. One night, very late, he reads another interview given by the famous rapper, in which the lunatic actually gives him credit for making the collages. The rapper doesn't know his last name, because Henrik never posted it to the online gallery, but nonetheless his first name gets out there. Gossip columnists refer to him as an artist and a recluse. He becomes a mystery or a theoretical presence, an entity the rapper spoke into existence.

One evening the foreman knocks on his cabin door and escorts him off the ship. I don't know, he says when Henrik asks why. I asked and they wouldn't tell me. Henrik rides a motorboat driven by a kid in a junior sailor's jacket all the way to shore. During the ride, he turns a couple times to look at the wake churning the surface and, beyond it, the setting sun, which he hasn't seen in at least a month. He climbs into the rear bench seat of a black Escalade parked near the dock. The first two benches are occupied by petty officers who don't speak as they scrutinize or ignore him. The SUV circles the streets of Nome and stops at the only coffee shop in town. Henrik is told to get out and go order whatever he wants inside. One of the officers, the one in plainclothes whose name is Walsh or Welsh, follows him in while the rest wait in the vehicle. Henrik and this ordinary looking man talk about his collages. They lament the sad truth of plastics in the ocean, the havoc wrought on fisheries and other wildlife communities by human industry, the abject strangeness of his new and blurry connection to the famous rapper. The officer only takes a sip or two from his decaf. He seems more content to watch Henrik drink tea and eat a blueberry muffin. They are the only customers in the place. At some point, not long before closing, the cashier locks her drawer and moves over to the gift shop and starts to wipe down the counter and dust the knick knacks on the shelves, as if the two of them are ghosts or do not exist. The officer leans in close and asks whether Henrik knows that things are always happening in the background, if he has ever heard of the W54 nuclear warhead, the smallest ever to be officially developed for the American arsenal. He asks whether Henrik is aware of the hostile nations around the globe that are speeding toward their own apocalyptic discoveries and mean to destabilize and ultimately eradicate the power of the United States and the glory of being an American. He asks whether Henrik has any knowledge of the history of the United States government's support for the arts, even those that ostensibly communicate anti-industrialist themes, and if he knows about the many fish consumption scenarios the human mind can conceive, or that fish and their insides can be soldiers. This Welsh or Walsh fellow leans in even closer, wrapping one hairy fist around the other, and asks if Henrik understands that he is not so mysterious, there are people aside from the officer speaking to him who know exactly who he is and where he can be found, and whether he can accept the terms of the following proposal, which in all reality he probably should.

[38]

Bioliberals are social democrats who embrace biotechnology and the new values that this entails. They live in a world where the hype of synthetic biology has come true and delivered on its promises—a society in symbiosis with the natural world. Biology is at the centre of their world-view, leading to a radically different technological landscape to our own. Nature is enhanced to meet growing human needs, but people also adjust their needs to match available resources. Each person produces their own energy according to their needs. Bioliberals are essentially farmers, cooks and gardeners. Not just of plants and food, but of products too. Gardens, kitchens and farms replace factories and workshops.

[http://unitedmicrokingdoms.org/bioliberals/]

[39]

Travelers commonly pull off on the Utah side of Wendover to gaze out at the Bonneville Salt Flats, a geological oddity monumentalized by the world speed records that have been set and broken across its crystalline labyrinths of sodium chloride. The extreme speeds of modified vehicles like the Turbinator II contrast to a maximal degree with the imperceptible gradations of geological time, all sense of passage and procession is distorted.

[40]

Oksana, 36, is an amateur submarine technician and suboceanic cartographer. For now she lives on the Kwajalein Atoll of the Ralik Chain of the Republic of the Marshall Islands. Her apartment is small and sparse, one in a line of identical rooms in a small stucco building with red doors and a flat roof. She moved to the North Pacific in 2015 after the reemergence of fascism in her home country of Poland—embodied by the League of Polish Families, the European National Front, the International Third Position, and other extremist groups— finally became unbearable, stifling her scholarly activities and rendering an internationalist worldview increasingly untenable [at least in public]. Most of the people here are American military personnel. The Marshall Islanders speak English as a general rule. As such, that is what she speaks both in the home and in public. The grassy area behind her room is strewn with tools, panels of metal, thermal polymers, buckets caked with the sedimented concretions of various high tensile waterproof sealants, different assemblies of scaffolding, coils of wire and cable, motors from a range of vehicles [e.g. riding lawnmowers, golf carts, and dune buggies], and other mechanical paraphernalia, most of which she has acquired through her husband, Derek, a rogue cryptologist at the Ronald Reagan Ballistic Missile Defense Test Site [RTS] down the street. The work of an undersea cartographer is awkward and dangerous in a militarized zone. After the sun sets, which she watches from the kitchen window every evening, because the blood-red aureole sinking in the west never ceases to remind her of her home country's flag, she backs the grain truck, a relic manufactured in the early 1960s, out of the small garage assigned to her and Derek's lodging unit and drives it three blocks to the crumbling cement boat landing at the beach. She pulls back the canvas sheet and unloads the submarine from the truck bed, resting it in the small lapping ebbs of the surf. The submarine is flat and narrow, designed to look something like a hardshell surfboard case. It allows her enough room to turn her head and move her arms, so that she can navigate, peer out the portholes, and jot coordinates in her cartographer's log and sometimes sketch the more poignant or sublime sights within the underwater environment. After unloading, she climbs back up into the driver's seat and pulls the truck into the vacant parking lot, then walks back down the sloping sand. She slides into the contraption on her back, reaches skyward for the open hatch, and pulls it closed. Entombed in her homemade device, she powers the propellers and submerges under the darkening sea.

Kwajalein is one of the large atolls comprising the Pacific Proving Grounds, a political zone invented by the United States where key institutions within the military-industrial complex detonated more than 100 nuclear bombs between the years 1946 and 1962. As of this writing [24 January 2020] many of the islands, reefs, atolls, and waters are still contaminated from the fallout of these tests. The indigenous populations are ensured of an increased risk of cancers as a result of exposure to ionized radiation—that which they breathed in the hours after detonation, that which is known to have lingered in various forms as late as the 1970s, and, perhaps, that which they pass to subsequent generations in the form of a mutated genome.

One morning, Oksana fetches the mail from the box at the end of the drive. Among bills, announcements, and coupons to local businesses, she finds an English language paperback edition of a novel titled *Nocilla Experience*. The author is named Fernández Mallo. It is not wrapped. There is nothing to indicate where it has come from. She takes it inside, and without intending, reads it through to the end. Not so much an epiphany as a dispositional shift, she feels a long suspicion suddenly confirmed: she has no clue what a nation is.

[41]

The myth discussed here comes together in one simple declaration of faith: "information is a natural object." No myth worth its weight in salt would consent, however, to exist in such an abbreviated form. Besides, what is a "natural object"? Everyone knows and uses the words *natural* and *object*, but most of us don't bother asking what they really mean or how we use them. The people who like asking such questions are mostly philosophers. But they are very much at odds with one another about what nature (or "the natural") is. Even the question of whether we should talk about nature with or without a definitive article—in German, the difference between *Natur* and *die Natur*—separates those who believe that there is a single nature, independent of its conceptualization of human beings, of which humanity forms a part, from the camp that thinks that nature should only be talked about as an adjective, hence *natural.* And *natural* is of course a word with many, many meanings, as one gathers from this list of incongruous opposites: *artificial, technical, artistic, spiritual, civilized, affected, contrived, unhealthy,* and so on.

Peter Janich, *What is Information?*, trans. Eric Hayot & Lea Pao

[42]

One sees these old VW Microbuses cruising along the beaches of Southern California, sunshine glinting off the polished body and the surfboards strapped to the luggage rack, or parked beside a crackling bonfire around which its carefree riders form a circle, play the guitar, and sing, and recalls the romance of the American counterculture of the 1960's. The images of tanned young people, flower children, and free love efface the vehicle's postwar origins, when Dutch importer Ben Pon observed a small industrial vehicle called the Plattenwagen in Wolfsburg, marveled at the simplicity of its design, and surmised a more capable machine immanent in its lines. The Microbus was conceived more or less as a mobile storage container—a steel box fixed to the chassis of the Beetle, Hitler's "people's car," for the express purpose of moving parts across the floors of West German factories, thus doing its part for the integration of the young country into the global economy of the future. In general usage, they are great for coasting, just as Silvia and Rafael do now, she rides on the passenger side of the front bench seat as he drives and hums. They are just north of Lake Tahoe, heading toward Reno where they will pick up Highway 50 all the way to Moab. Silvia tries to sleep but can't. Billy the Kid's stalemate sculpture weighs the seat between them. It's so damn hot, she says. Her toes struggle in her Army boots. She takes them off and rolls the cuffs of her jeans. A sloping embankment abuts the freeway on the right, scattered with short scrub bushes and spalls of native rock. Near the top of the ridge, just below the jagged frontier where mountain and sky appear to touch, a row of power lines strings among the Ponderosas, drawing her eye into the distance. For small moments that end as quickly as they open, she feels as if her gaze, the roadway, the Microbus, the mountain itself all converge—because in certain ways they do. Ahead, shrouded in a haze of sunshine that is a wonder in itself given the absolute cloudlessness of the afternoon, the last visible post stands at the peak of a long declivity. From this distance it reminds her of *Christ the Redeemer* in Rio de Janeiro, a statue she has never seen outside of photographs and video footage in a place she has never visited—one of the New7Wonders of the World. She read once [a report confirmed by a cousin who had gone to Rio during the Olympics, but not as a spectator of the games] that tourists access the site by a small train line that runs from the base of the Corcovado all the way to the conical peak, where the *Redeemer* is located, and which juts into the sky like the bow of a ship frozen in the terrible process of foundering. They gather there like pilgrims, photographing the mighty Christ, some praying or breaking down into ecstatic sobs. In this way, the Corcovado is connected to the Sierra Nevada through which the Microbus coasts and turns, the site of the famed American gold rush of the mid-nineteenth century. Thousands journeyed here from the eastern seaboard and western frontier with the goal of striking it rich and liberating their family lineages from the constraints of stagnant European pasts—practitioners of the widely held theory stating it is the land that makes the American. Every few miles, a sign appears on the side of the interstate advertising a tour of some recovered gold mine and, with it, the chance to recreate the life of an old prospector. Rafael reaches for the bottle of Coke in the cup holder and takes a large, stinging swig. He fears the future in the same way Silvia fears the past. They had sat up very late the night she arrived in San Francisco, sipping from tall cans of Yerba Mate. Rafael smoked half a pack of clove cigarettes laced with marijuana and talked about the coming resource shortages and the global pandemic of guerilla sectarianism that would result. His stopovers at the Black Rose were a needed but temporary repose. Among their luggage and coolers are the Geiger and scintillation counters, potassium iodide tablets branded *ThyroSafe*, HAZMAT suits [if needed], instructional manuals for beginners and advanced amateurs alike, and maps of the abandoned mines of Moab, Utah—at one point, a perfect century after the peak of the California gold rush, the self-proclaimed Uranium Capital of the World. He goes to sleep every night dreaming about the return of the hydrogen bomb. He wants to be ahead of it, one of the new-age industrialists extracting and hoarding precious resources from the earth. The tools reveal who we are, he had said. They open the soil and show us our greatest fears.

[43]

The side of a smooth green hill, torn by floods, may at first very properly be called deformed, and on the same principle, though not with the same impression, as a gash on a living animal. When the rawness of such a gash in the ground is softened, and in part concealed and ornamented by the effects of time, and the progress of vegetation, deformity, by this usual process, is converted into picturesqueness; and this is the case with quarries, gravel pits, etc., which at first are deformities, and which in their most picturesque state, are often considered as such by the levelling improver.

[44]

A total of 36,560 people died on the nation's roads in 2018.

Associated Press

One night Pancho walks past the Target on 4th & Mission Street, a block from the San Francisco Museum of Modern Art. The store closes at 1:00 a.m. He enters at 12:45 and fills a cart with everything he can reach or, in some cases, lift. Items pile up and spill onto the floor. When he is finished, he pushes the cart through the sliding glass partition into the world outside. No one tries to stop him. No one calls out. The Target is an Express location built on the ground floor of a hybrid retail/residential unit, a mutation of the old arrangement by which a proprietor would live above his shop, initiated by the demands of a sophisticated consumer culture. At some point he passes in and out of the notion that he lives in the store. He returns most nights for a month or two, wearing neither shoes nor shirt, pushing the cart beneath the glowing white lights, what he believes to be a soothing phosphorescence, while the people in the apartments above him sleep. The employees watch him like zombies, they are underpaid and indifferent or maybe cheer him on or gaze at him in semi-conscious awe, stoned into another realm of existence. He follows no ready made path through the aisles, bakery, pharmacy, and produce sections. The only rule is that he must not begin in the same place on consecutive nights. He fills the cart with perishables and nonperishables, as well as household and bodily apparel—breakfast cereals, yogurts, juices, multivitamins, tampons, disinfectants, detergents, lunch meats, t-shirts, running shoes, windshield wipers, dumbbells, ottomans, throw pillows, coffee makers, on and on, aiming to exhaust every permutation latent in the store's index of goods. He pushes the cart to a storage container on 10th & Howard that he rents in lieu of a permanent residence. Tonight, he finishes by placing a plastic fern on top of a bucket of kettle corn. He takes a picture of the half-full storage container with his phone and uploads it to the various image boards on which sections of his manifesto appear. Perhaps due to the slow accumulation of goods, a shifting formation that is always dead on arrival, or the rancid smell of old produce, he finds this to be the purest method of charting one's existence in this world. At some point people from his following start to show up. They want to purchase his artifacts. He sells them at an enormous profit.

[46]

HANTRU 1 is a small stretch of the global suboceanic fiberoptic cable system used to transmit nearly the entire load of international internet traffic. It originates in the U.S.-organized territory of Guam and runs east as far as Majuro, branching south to the Federated States of Micronesia and north to the outlying atolls of the Marshall Islands, specifically Kwajalein. HANTRU 1 is enclosed in a steel pipeline skimmed here and there with reefs and barnacles and various mineral deposits making shapes for which no precise name exists. The cable itself is a mere fiber no wider than an ordinary garden hose.

Franco "Bifo" Birardi:

> Let's call the infosphere the *universe of transmitters*, and the *social brain* the universe of receivers. The *universe of receivers*—human beings made of flesh, and frail and sensuous organs—is not formatted according to the standards of digital transmitters. So what happens? As the electronic universe of transmission interfaces with the organic world of reception, it is producing pathological effects: panic, over-excitement, hyperactivity, attention deficit disorders, dyslexia, information overload, and the saturation of neural circuitry.

HANTRU 1 is approximately 3,000 kilometers in length. It is a miniscule appendage of a global immensity. One may draw the analogy between the suboceanic cable network and the *neural circuitry* of an individual brain, even though such a comparison is said to rely on conflicting systems. This is perhaps the "hive-mind" much discussed in works of fantasy and science-fiction. Oksana was raised in the countryside near Łódź. The city is known regionally for its former prolificacy in the manufacture of fabrics. This golden age is enshrined in the Central Museum of Textiles, which houses machinery and craftworks dating from the nineteenth century. Oksana never once visited this museum, nor does she know of its existence. The industry was reduced to relics and images well before the time of her birth. She is wholly unaware of her home city's former commercial prowess. Her father was a line worker intermittently employed by the municipal government. Her mother was a teacher. Oksana spent her childhood assisting her grandfather [maternal] on the family's small dairy farm. She would milk cows early in the morning, go to school during the daytime, and laze in the pastures all afternoon, watching the clouds and birds pass above the power lines. She imagined an invisible shaft linking everything crossing that vertical infinity to the biological mechanisms of her eyesight. After dinner, while her parents cleaned the kitchen and read the newspaper, she retreated to the cozy back yard, where her grandfather rested in an old rocking chair beside the vegetable garden after returning from market. She sat at his feet and listened to stories of his boyhood, how he too would go to school and milk the cows and chase calves in the lilting grasses. When his mood was gray, or if he had already consumed his vodka, he would tell her of the Nazi invasion of their homeland and the establishment of the Łódź Ghetto, which was the second largest in all of Nazi-occupied Europe. Incarcerated Jews and Roma functioned as a forced labor reserve. They were made to convert the old textile factories into German munitions plants. In this way, they were obliged to participate in their own immiseration. As he recited tales of violence and misery, he would sometimes point at a ditch or mound in the distance past the cow pen and describe what had happened there, the pounding noise of Wehrmacht machine guns, bombs, and mortar shells, the sickening odor of black powder mixed with blood, the frenzy of screams and lowing, the scars, craters, and lacerations disfiguring the landscape. When she came of age, she got the idea of countering the Nazi invasion by crossing into Germany. She found herself fascinated by borders and their tendency to both cause and respond to political upheaval. She studied geography at TU Darmstadt through the university's Institut für Angewandte Geowissenschaften, acquired proficiency in the latest GIS methods, got bored with the strictures of formal academic practice, dropped out, and found sporadic freelance work updating tourist maps of German cities for the reunified Federal Ministry for Economic Affairs and Energy. At some point she met Derek, who was stationed at the American military base. It was around this time that she first came across a reference to the suboceanic cable system, a footnote in a book about trans Pacific trade routes in the expanding colonial world. She thinks frequently of the Fernández Mallo book, specifically a passage in the "clarifications" provided by the author after the conclusion of the semi-fictional hybrid narrative in the American edition published by one of the multinational book conglomerates in New York City. Fernández Mallo reproduces the entire text of a letter he had received from a friend ["David Torres"], in which Torres expresses his concern over a similarity between one of Fernández Mallo's characters and one of Bolaño's from the monumental tome, 2666: "In the Bolaño novel, in Part Two, there's a guy who hangs math books from his clothesline to give the ideas an airing. Your character uses almost the exact same phrases as him. I'm guessing you haven't read the book but it's one of those ideas which will either fuck you over or, as Borges would say, which make up a secret order." Fifty meters beneath the surface, Oksana's phone does not get internet reception. Ironically, of course—HANTRU 1 being right there in front her.

[47]

I am just looking at the world, that's all. Anyone alive who had enough food and shelter, even 10 thousand years ago, would start observing the sky and would want somehow to demarcate the things that were happening. It is a basic human desire. I don't think one needs to know anything about astronomy. I call up the astronomers and give them the latitude and the longitude, and I say, What do you think? What if you had an unobstructed horizon? What is the angle for the solstice? Then they figure that out. Or I ask, What can I do with the moon that would be constant? And they say, Well, the extreme positions are every 18.61 years. That kind of cyclical time is very interesting to me, although I am aware that even that changes. For example, Stonehenge does not work accurately any more. The North Star, Polaris, has not always been the North Star and will not always be the North Star. So that even when we think in celestial terms, there is still indefiniteness.

Nancy Holt, JS-C Interview

[48]

The next morning, Hideki snaps photos of their hotel room. He aims his camera at the cactus print bedspreads and the framed paintings of pioneer wagon trains hanging over the headboards. The artist is local, the works embarrassing. After breakfast, he and Yasuko drive into the mountains and hike a trail overlooking the Salt Lake Valley. In one of the many photographs from this outing [most have been misplaced somewhere along the way], Yasuko can be seen in especially vivid detail from head to toe. She is backgrounded by open sky and, near the middle of the frame, the western edge of the young suburbs. The Great Salt Lake is not visible. Two rows of hawthorn bushes line the trail, lending a compositional symmetry to her simple pose. She stands with her hands crossed at the waist, showcasing the small gold wristwatch Hideki purchased as an anniversary gift the year before. Her legs mirror the fold of her hands, one foot placed slightly in front of the other with a small bend in the knee. She is wearing white and brown Oxfords, orange pants, a yellow tie-front blouse with a pattern of falling citrus fruit, and a blue handkerchief knotted at the hairline, slightly off center. She is not exactly smiling. Her lips are closed and turn vaguely upward—possibly an acknowledgement of the camera, or maybe a response to the intensity of the July sun still rising behind Hideki's shoulder. The black & white film suppresses how truly colorful her appearance seems to him, especially in coordination with the trail's many shades of brown and red, the different greens and yellows infusing the vegetation, and the uniform blue of the sky. He wonders whether her clothing, the temporary stillness of her body, its relation to both earth and atmosphere, somehow stores, radiates, and amplifies the rays of the sun. This proliferating sense of color is the thing he carries with him. Every time he digs out the photograph, whatever his reason for doing so might be, he finds it wholly unable to recreate this chromatic unity, which is entirely clear in his recollections. At times this failure of the image seems to him an egregious violation of his memory—the destruction of a moment that cannot be regained. His eyes often project color onto the ink and paper, so that for miniscule slices in time he sees Yasuko as she existed in that moment, as if he is standing again on that high trail among trees with the sun warming his back. He can remember every individual stone, every vein of every leaf, every hair on her arms, so thin they are almost translucent… One night in the mid 70's, returning very late from a visit to an old friend, he opens a bottle of Coors and sits on the couch for a while, waiting for the sun to rise. At some point he pulls the photo from its place in the album. He looks into Yasuko's eyes, she simply seems very far away…

[49]

The Great Basin is the most northerly of the four American deserts. Unlike the other three, which have almost exclusive ties to warm-temperate and tropical/subtropical vegetation types, the Great Basin has affinities with cold-temperate vegetation. The Chihuahuan and Sonoran deserts may in fact be more closely related to the Argentine "Monte" than they are to the Great Basin (Turner 1994).

[https://www.worldwildlife.org/ecoregions/na1305]

Leo later learns that Martha's most recent message arrived a week after she had sent it. The lag interval strikes him as crucially informative, because it reveals the retrospective nature of their relationship, which, he suspects, is how the overwhelming majority of things on earth appear— retrospectively—although he has no way to prove it. She tells him of the trip she took with her mother to the United States. They spent several days in Hollywood followed by a week in Las Vegas. Her mother doesn't gamble, Martha wrote, and she hates the desert. Nonetheless she wanted to see the bright lights of the strip from high above. They got a room on the twenty-eighth floor of the Paris Las Vegas with a perfect view of the *Eiffel Tower Experience*. The windows didn't open because of all the suicides people would commit if they did. From that high up, the flows of cars and people between buildings looked very much like silent diagrams of the casino floors, the tourists like multivalent electrons whose movements formed bonds among different parts of the city. Their time alternated between sleeping, eating at buffets, shopping, and looking down at the street level circuitry after the sun had set. The only things to read in the hotel room were brochures for local attractions, the programs and messages of the television, and the *Book of Mormon* left at some point by the Latter Day Saints. She got out of bed very late one night unable to sleep, maybe because in that city the middle of the night is hardly discernible from high noon. She went down to the strip, intending to circle the block and go back to bed. She wound up getting lost and wandering for several hours. Every so often she reached a street corner and saw the tip of the Eiffel Tower from a new angle. She would make a mental note of its proximity and direction, take the moving walkways among tourists from all parts of the world to where she thought it was, and would find herself in some new place on the strip just as far from her hotel as she had been already. To orient herself and perhaps ask for directions, she entered a 24-hour bookshop. She didn't even make it to the counter, because her attention was immediately drawn to a display table in the very front of the store. Specifically, she was attracted to a box set of novels propped on a plexiglass stand. *Nocilla Trilogy*, it said, a title that was somewhat familiar to her given its European reference point, even though she herself was not Spanish and had never eaten Nocilla nor heard of the trilogy's author, let alone read anything he had written. She picked it up and admired the clarity of the design, a cream colored box with the title centered at the top, separated by a thin black line from the author's name, which was printed in a slightly larger and very simple sans-serif font. Beneath that was a column of three outlined images resembling petroglyphs or emojis, she couldn't decide. On top was a lavender cloud, then a sea-green sunset, and finally, at the bottom, a salmon-colored flame. The whole thing was shrink-wrapped and reflected the blinking lights penetrating the glass storefront. I didn't even need to read the books to know that I loved them, her message says. I felt as if their elegant design contained everything I needed to know. She purchased them and forgot to ask for directions to the hotel, yet somehow, cradling the box set against her chest, she found her way back. She rode the elevator to the twenty-eighth floor and secluded herself in the bathroom while her mother slept. The books were clearly numbered 1, 2, and 3. Even so she decided to begin with the last in the spirit of her inverted afternoon. I was cast out to sea, she said. Reading it felt like a vacation within my vacation, a journey to another place just as strange and unrealistic as Las Vegas. She described a recurring scene in which the narrator, a slightly fictionalized version of the author, related a nearly identical journey of bewilderment through the high voltage streets of Las Vegas, which included his own midnight book purchase from what might have been the same 24-hour shop. He also had never heard of the author of the book he bought, a man named Paul Auster, so of course he had never read *The Music of Chance*, and neither had the woman with whom he shared a hotel room, a cool and distant person he loved madly and called La Maga. I looked up from my reading and gazed frequently at myself in the mirror while holding the book open, Martha's message says, and I discovered that I could not distinguish the moments of reading from the moments of looking up.

Among the many sections in Leo's unending novel, six dramatize portions of the land artist Robert Smithson's 1967 *Artforum* essay, "A Tour of the Monuments of Passaic, New Jersey." The first one goes like this:

Robert goes to the Port Authority Building on 41st Street and 8th Avenue. He lingers for a few minutes at a news stand, picks up a copy of the Times and, on a whim, a Signet paperback called Earthworks *by a guy named Aldiss. It's a Saturday, he doesn't have anything else to do, he's seen pretty much everything there is to see around here, seen it and thought about it and documented it in his way. Gets a ticket to Passaic, heads upstairs to the bus terminal (platform 173), and rides the no. 30 bus of the Inter-City Transportation Company down Highway 2.*

Moving a 1,000-Pound Sculpture Can be a Fine Work of Art, Too. If you don't look where you're going in Manhattan's art belt these days, you might trip over (or at least brush past) a $30,000 marble sculpture, a bunch of exotic face masks or a Cezanne or six.

Down Orient Way in Rutherford. He compares the sky over suburban New Jersey to the sky he reads about in the Aldiss book; the one a clear cobalt blue, the other a "great black and brown shield on which moisture gleamed." The book seems like it is about a soil shortage on a future earth. He gets bored, packs it in his rucksack, and gazes out the window at the passing monuments. The day is unseasonably warm and perfect. Sunlight still lasts long into evening. His knees begin to jostle, he is getting that familiar impulse to see. He will sit this way, restlessly, seven years after his trip to Passaic; he will feel this need to touch the earth, which he cannot help but view conceptually, riding in the sky above the Amarillo desert.

In New Jersey, he pulls the buzzer cord. He must drop down and touch the soil with his feet. He takes the plunge out the collapsing bus door. He stops at a bridge, Instamatic pointing, the fist line of Aldiss caught in his head: "The dead man drifted along in the breeze."

Soon after Leo reads Martha's message, the third Fernández Mallo book, titled *Nocilla Lab*, appears in general delivery with her return address written in the corner of the envelope. He is stunned to see the Smithson essay quoted in its middle section when he finally opens it more than a month later. He eventually falls asleep on the floor beside the child, and as he drifts away he becomes entangled in the question of whether thinking happens in order to build dreams or destroy them, to ease flows or demolish existing channels. He dreams of the certain resemblances between the Las Vegas strip, the Russian steppe, and the circuitry inside his phone.

[51]

[In the American desert] may spring up new and mongrel races, like new formations in geology, the amalgamation of the "debris" and "abrasions" of former races, civilized and savage; the remains of broken and almost extinguished tribes; the descendants of wandering hunters and trappers; of fugitives from the Spanish and American frontiers; of adventurers and desperadoes of every class and country yearly ejected from the bosom of society into the wilderness.

Washington Irving

[52]

Sometime after his final visit to the Black Rose, Romano crosses north at Tecate. As usual, the CBP agent, who he has seen before, asks if he has anything to declare. Nothing except myself, he says, and a couple bottles of Mezcal. Gifts for my friends. The agent asks to look in his trunk, which is empty except for a spare tire, lug wrench, and flimsy jack. He leaves a wake of black exhaust as he coasts north. A week earlier Saavedra left Mexico unannounced. At first Romano figured he had gone to stay with a girlfriend or to Tijuana, although the two possibilities were probably one in the same. In the middle of the night, his phone rang. It's me, Saavedra said. Romano asked what was up. Saavedra was silent for a while. Romano dozed off to the sound of the big man's breathing. Eventually Saavedra apologized. I have some things to take care of in the States. I'm in California. I'm heading to Nevada tomorrow. I think I might stay a night or two at Tahoe first. He asked Romano if he understood the fact that everything happens in slow motion, and if he did understand this fact, could he fathom its significance. The human is a fragile and tragically limited creature. It cannot detect the speed at which events truly occur. If it could, the entire species would die from unholy despair. That's why things overlap, he said. That's why you can't get those bodies out of your head. They're still dying even though they are buried and rotting. You hear the innocent laughter that breaks through the bursts of terror. Romano asked him what the fuck he was going on about. It's too early for this, or too late, the investigator said. What time is it, anyway? Have you turned into a lunatic overnight? Saavedra apologized again. At some point he hung up. Romano said his friend's name, Aurelio, then said it again either to verify that the line had severed or to recover the big man's voice from the silence. He ponders that silence as the sun blasts through the windshield of his piece of shit car. The desert produces the illusion of monotony. Every rock and bit of scrub might be the next one, or the last one he passed. He stops in El Centro to fill up at a Shell Station and to eat at a Burger King before turning north. He feels Mexicali on the other side of the border, reflecting God's truths. As he eats he wonders how the town and the highway cutting through it came to be. Every single building appears to have blown in on the wind, everything is coated in ochre dust, possibly made from it—not unlike a mining town from the nineteenth century, a cobbling of shacks put on stilts, built in anticipation of its inevitable dismemberment. A storm might rise and sweep it away.

Slab City is overflowing with tourists and influencers, people in their twenties who dress like flower children and livestream their adventures dealing in VW Microbuses, sculptures of junk, and the painted rocks. He parks in the dust and hoists his duffel bag from the back seat, setting it on his lap. He takes a long pull from one of the Mezcal bottles, replaces it in the bag, and pushes through the crowds. A mile or so east of Slab City he reaches a dirt road running parallel to an irrigation canal that continues all the way to the border. Some noises from the distant crowds reach him on the wind. Voices that talk to him, voices that rise from the earth and whisper fragments of his name. He lights a cigar and trudges further north, fanning himself with the lapels of his raincoat and sweating from the unrelenting heat. Eventually he glimpses an Airstream a couple hundred yards off the road. The trailer looks like an unearthed bomb shelter, or maybe just a bomb. It always inspires a sense of looming disaster, especially from a distance, not necessarily because it suggests a mass mortality event, which it does, but because when looking at it he always gets the feeling that he has fallen into a pre-ordered routine or ritual, a set of codes that has consumed him and animated his body, and that whether he wanted to or not, he could never move or think in any other way, a zombie drifting across the sand. As usual, Frankie Reál sits in his wheelchair beside a plastic lawn table in the shade of a blue awning, gazing toward the canal. If it isn't Pat Garret himself, Reál says. Romano mumbles something as he sets the duffel bag on the table, then pulls out the bottles of Mezcal and a wad of cash. I think I might have something, he says. He peels a couple bills off the wad and hands them to Reál, who takes them smiling and slides them folded into his breast pocket. I just want to check it out first, Romano says, get your opinion. He also pulls out a laptop, which he sets between the bottles, as if preparing for an event somewhere between a party and a seminar. They sip Mezcal and discuss the missing woman's files and browsing history and her breadcrumb trails of content until they both believe to see the blurry edges of a pattern emerge. She liked to frequent a set of deep web image boards populated with slivers of conspiracies mostly about the desert, which is like a gathering of secret nations or a massive QR code, or about missing persons who suddenly appear in inappropriate places, or soap commercials foretelling 9/11 all the way back in the early days of television. There are lists of demands, alternate histories dating to the supercontinents Vaalbara and Ur, something called the Paraboloid Microkingdom. They come across a treatise on guerilla marketing, apparently founded on an aborted Hasbro Industries initiative from the 60's that had tried to incorporate the found-object theory of art and aesthetics, a form of Dada advertising, and the natural human desire for desire itself. Romano sets up a line of Campbell's Soup cans in the dirt while Reál grills hamburgers. During dinner they finish the first bottle of Mezcal, open the second, and afterwards take turns firing the Desert Eagle .44 Magnum at the cans. You're getting pretty good with that thing, Reál notes.

[53]

We went outside and looked up at the sky and saw many planes.

Minoru Sumida, Survivor of the Atomic Bombing of
Hiroshima City, describing his experience of Pearl Harbor,
Interviewed by Shinpei Takeda, Feb.18-20, 2008, Honolulu,
HI, [*Hiroshima Nagasaki Download,* https://youtu.be/
TTfVBftFMNY]

[54]

Stan and John Bearheart split a six pack on the hood of the pickup. They have nothing much to do other than watch tourists photograph the salt flats. These people form small clusters on the dusty slope beyond the parking lot, squeezing together so as to all be visible in the frames of their cameras. A few ask nearby strangers to snap a picture of their group. Some take turns photographing each other. One tries again and again to perfect the view of the selfie-stick. A large family of Mormon fundamentalists, marked by their wool coats, bonnets, and gingham dresses, stare into the distance with their backs to the highway. They perhaps watch two wanderers, two small pinpoints, stray far across the pan. These drifters might be insane, they might be radicals of some kind seeking eternity in the horizon. Stan uses the urinal in the rest stop men's room. The sink is out of order. When he returns, the shadow figures are no longer visible. He reads out loud: *All materials, all objects, everything we see, are clots—catastrophes that took place on the neutral, two-dimensional, isotropic plane coterminous with The Beginning. These are the so-call First Order Catastrophes. When a foreign agent alters the equilibrium of one of these objects, it then breaks off in unpredictable directions, dragging along other objects— whether near or far—in a kind of domino effect. This we call a Second Order Catastrophe. The desert, given its flatness and isotropic nature, is the least catastrophic place* [Fernández Mallo, *Nocilla Dream*]. The distant wanderers are visible once again. He cannot tell whether they are coming or going, or if they are standing still. Perhaps they were lying on their backs, gazing up at the immensity of electrons filling all layers of the planet's atmosphere, and have now risen on legs which may be shaky and unstable from the afternoon heat [the temperature, according to the weather app on John Bearheart's iPhone, approaches forty-three degrees Celsius]—a repetition, or even better, a homotypic fusion with the first forms of bipedal life ascending from the soil.

[55]

Albert Speer said that oil had been a major factor in the decision to invade the Soviet Union. Hitler believed that Baku's oil resources were essential for the survival of the Third Reich, as a dearth of oil resources was a vulnerability of Germany's military.

[https://en.wikipedia.org/wiki/Operation_Barbarossa]

[56]

At some point a market develops. Anonymous followers start filling the grounds around his storage container with their own waste products. Items wash up, dredged from homes as salmon are harvested from the sea. Of course he sells these, as well. He pushes his cart to the facility one Saturday and finds a stack of daily *San Francisco Chronicle*s from December 1968 to October 1969, many of them containing front page headlines about the Zodiac Killer. The next week, in addition to the newspapers, he finds a complete oak bedroom set and a library of home movies recorded on VHS tapes. Things accumulate, more and more. Boxes of floppy drives, obsolete gaming consoles, cell phones too old to function in existing cellular networks, sofa cushions, bundles of scarves and stocking caps, a Geiger counter welded to a metal detector perhaps in some arcane political or aesthetic statement, guitars with and without strings, keyboards, coffee mugs, china sets seemingly complete and incomplete, empty milk jugs, an antique washboard, at least two dozen pre-electric clothes irons, a stack of power strips arranged in a model of the Eiffel Tower, twenty-five or more milk crates filled with country-western albums from the 60's and 70's, a gourd painted gold and black, medical records and death certificates, a pine cabinet jammed tight with German Lugers that may or may not have been replicas [they were packed too tightly to withdraw one for inspection]. At some point he finds the stripped chassis of a pickup-truck or a muscle car. The next week a semi-trailer is parked beside the container, its hatch rolled open and exposing a displaced living room—sofa, chairs, rug, end tables, side lamps all summoning him to have tea with the owner, who of course is nowhere to be found. He comes to feel every week as if he is entering the bombed-out remnants of an abandoned war zone, that he is the great sifter salvaging and assigning value to the carrion of a vanished society.

One night, he finds a person at the bin leaning against the semi-trailer, smoking a pungent cigar in the shadows. He assumes it is the owner of the storage bins, there to receive his half of the profits from Pancho's sales, but as he walks closer he figures the guy for a cop. Pawn division? he says. The person is thinly built, much shorter than Pancho himself. He wears unlaced desert boots, a khaki suit, a crumpled raincoat. A density of shadows conceals his face. Nope, he says. I'm not the pawn brigade. I wish I was, but no, I'm not. He tosses the cigar onto a pile of Atari cartridges edging the storage container. He clears his throat. In a raspy tenor he addresses Pancho by his legal name. Come on, the person says [the accent is Brooklyn or maybe Bronx], let's take a ride.

They walk together into darkness. A ridiculous car idles in the golden-yellow glow of a streetlamp on the other side. For a moment Pancho mistakes it for a piece of junk someone had left. Despite his nervousness or because of it, he erupts in laughter, perhaps the laughter of the insane. He is certain that the rusted body and treadless tires are an image from the future, that he has been liberated, which is to say better connected, and that despite standing here he gazes at the vehicle, himself, and the investigator across a long and dusty expanse, the paradox of distant proximity or proximate distance that one falls into late at night, unmotivated, when switching channels on their television.

[57]

The Anarcho-evolutionists abandon most technologies, or at least stop developing them, and concentrate on using science to maximise their own physical capabilities through training, DIY biohacking and self-experimentation. They believe that humans should modify themselves to exist within the limits of the planet rather than modifying the planet to meet their ever growing needs. There are a high number of post-humanists amongst the Anarcho-evolutionists, individuals whose physiologies have been improved beyond that which is considered naturally human. They essentially take evolution into their own hands. Very little is regulated, citizens can do as they please as long as it doesn't harm anyone else.

[http://unitedmicrokingdoms.org/anarcho-evolutionists/]

[58]

Twenty years ago, no one could have imagined that in this vast wasteland of the California desert we would build fully realized cities with all of the urban services and none of the urban problems of America's metropolitan centers. To sell that idea is the secret of American success. To convince the public that this hot, parched land could be a suburban oasis was a feat that required not only imagination, but daring.

Robert Culp, playing Dr. Bart Keppel, renowned expert in consumer psychology, *Columbo*, s. 3 ep. 4, "Double Exposure," 1973

[59]

One day Oksana heads to the fish market on the other side of the lagoon. She does not find the usual bustle among tables of grouper, mullet, sea chub, soldierfish… In fact the fish mongers have not set up shop today at all. She inquires with an elderly woman selling daikon and eggplants from a wooden cart, repeating her question twice [Do you know why there are no fish today?] into the woman's ear. At home, she makes a salad of green papaya and shredded daikon with a soy-peanut-chile sauce. Derek eats most of it along with a 7 oz. can of Sea Queen Alaskan Salmon. The air strip ought to be considered one of the seven wonders of the world, he says after dinner, over the sound of a *Jeopardy* rerun [perhaps his comment is apropos of something Alex Trebek has said, Oksana has not been listening]. It's the first part of the world's growing exoskeleton, he says. Eventually, the entire planet will be encased in concrete, oceans and everything. You can thank the military-industrial complex for that. They want everything to be bomb-proof so they can keep developing their apocalyptic super weapons. They don't want to actually use them, they just want the defense contracts. They have to keep building and building. That's what makes the world go round. These fuckers believe in infinite growth. They actually think they'll live forever. He lights a Marlboro 100, works the lever of his reclining chair, his own exoskeleton, and leans back deeply in the blue light of television signals. They have sex before bed. Derek falls asleep almost immediately afterward with nothing on but athletic socks and an Army issued t-shirt. Oksana spends the next several hours at the kitchen table, searching the Internet. She finds an explanation for the missing fish on the Radio New Zealand website:

The latest US Army report confirms that fish in many locations on Kwajalein Island and nearby islands on the west side of the atoll contain dangerous levels of arsenic and PCBs—all seriously toxic chemicals.

"Cancer risk and non-cancer hazard are unacceptable for adult and child Marshallese residents under numerous evaluated fish consumption scenarios," said the report into the contamination of reef fish at the US Army Garrison-Kwajalein Atoll.

The contamination is the result mainly of waste from industrial vessel operations in the Army's port and leaching from the Kwajalein landfill that has contaminated reef fish in the area with toxic materials.

The report concluded that, reef fish consumption poses potentially unacceptable cancer risks to Marshallese adults and children who draw most of their reef fish from industrial (Kwajalein Harbor and Kwajalein landfill) and recreational areas (North Point, Ski Platform, American/Japanese pools) on Kwajalein Islet.

[https://www.rnz.co.nz/international/pacific-news/395041/
us-army-report-reef-fish-at-marshalls-atoll-are-toxic]

Later, she comes across a Reddit forum populated by practitioners and enthusiasts of suboceanic cartography. One particular thread catches her eye. A user asks whether anyone else has experienced the phenomenon of watching faces manifest in the lines of maps. This person mentions an arcane document titled *Orbis Typus Universalis Iuxta Hydrographorum Traditionem*, known more colloquially as the Stevens-Brown

Map, in which the author has overlaid a rudimentary world map with a network of crossing vectors, forming nodes at different points on land and at sea. According to the geographical description and cartobibliographic notes on the website of the John Carter Brown Library special collections archive, the map was made circa 1507 for a supplement to Ptolemy's *Geographia*, though for whatever reason was left out when the volume was published in 1513. It is thought to have been made by Martin Waldseemüller because of the particular woodblock from which it was printed. *First I see eyes*, this poster says, *then part of a nose, sometimes a mouth or jawline. I never see a whole face. Fragments come and go. Some of them have piercings, like punk rockers. Others look like they could belong to anyone on the street. Anybody have anything like this? Is this just matrixing? Am I nuts??* The majority of respondents answer in the affirmative. Two posts made seven months apart include identical links to the Wikipedia entry for the Bélmez Faces of Spain, which are said to appear in the walls and floor of an old cottage that is otherwise perfectly ordinary. Oksana vividly recalls the faces from the Fernández Mallo book, where the author mentions them multiple times, and, now that she has thought of it, from a TV documentary about Paranormal Europe she watched years ago, both in Germany and Poland. It seemed odd and miraculous that she would watch the low-budget affair once as a girl, then somehow see it again on a different station in a different country more than a decade later. Her memory now is of that original memory of having seen the film once before. Not a map, exactly, but still a strange recurrence.

Network infrastructure emerges through users' everyday practices. Depending on where they are in the world and the platform they are operating from, users activate and inhabit different slices of this wired infrastructure. In some locations the content they are seeking might be stored locally, and data has to travel only a short way between its origin and destination. Other content might have to circumnavigate the globe. In their engagements with certain forms of media, and in their differential activation of infrastructure, users are unknowingly entangled in specific kinds of infrastructural development. Through this process, changes in media practices aggregate to alter the economics, practices, temporality, and geography of undersea cable systems.

Nicole Starosielski, "Fixed Flow"

[60]

I feel that the need to look at the sky and at the moon and
stars is very basic, and it is inside all of us. So when I say my
work is an exteriorization of my own inner reality, I mean I
am giving back to people through art what they already have
in them.

Nancy Holt, JS-C Interview

[61]

We tried many things. I started to hide my scars when I came here. I thought that people might think this was contagious. I would not pass the military draft inspection because of this scar. When I took my clothes off, they asked…

I told them it was from the atomic bombing, then they shook their head and failed me. If the atomic bomb-related disease was to recur, the government would have to be responsible for its treatment. However, by then they already knew this could not be cured.

Minoru Sumida, [Hiroshima Nagasaki Download,
https://youtu.be/TTfVBftFMNY]

[62]

Several years after he had folded up the tripod on his Canon Reflex Zoom 8, after who knows what happens to the 64 ½ Mustang [it could be rusting in the desert, it could stand as the jewel in a rich man's collection], after he has given up the idea of filming time, because he no longer feels a need to document what is manifest in every atom of every surface, Hideki gets the idea to fill the yard with rose bushes. At first Yasuko is charmed by the care with which he tends them. She cradles the baby and watches from the deck as he clips the shears, uproots fistfuls of dandelion and bindweed [contagions which he comes to carp about with exhausting regularity], and rises occasionally to his feet in order to gaze upward at both his family and the sun, upon which he smiles, swigging from a glistening bottle of beer he keeps with him in the grass. For most of the spring and summer she assumes that he has consciously or unconsciously redirected his artistic desires to these rose bushes, which overflow with time, every afternoon that he puts into them returns exponentially in the volume of foliage and the intensity of pinks, whites, and reds saturating the velvety pedals. He must be some kind of a magician to make his plants grow this way. It's as if he wills them into life. There must be something in his blood.

One afternoon near the end of August, he comes inside, slides the glass door closed, and sits at the dining table with his face in his hands. He says nothing when Yasuko asks what is wrong. You're all dirty, she says. Maybe you'd feel better if you took a shower, whatever it is. Why don't you clean up. I'll put the baby to bed and we can discuss what's bothering you. At least take off your work gloves. The baby whimpers, and she hesitates to touch him on the shoulder. After several moments, he looks up. His face is unrecognizable. The features are his but somehow they do not belong to him. His eyes, cheeks, and lips twist into strange configurations, they give shape to the tortured expressions of people from another time. Ghosts appear and fade in every wrinkle, every line, every texture of the flesh. She removes her hand and steps back. A chill runs through her. I saw faces, he whispers, in the roses. Thousands of them. All at once. I could do nothing for them.

He showers after the sun sets and the light in their house dwindles to shadow. They eat dinner in front of the television and retire early to bed. The baby cries once or twice during the night.

OLD WORLD

A man named François Bernier once traveled around the globe experiencing the different peoples it contained. Based on a summary of his observations he proposed a new division of the earth according to the distribution of its inhabitants. He was a Frenchman born at Valanjou in Anjou. Valanjou was a former commune in Maine-et-Loire in the Loire Valley of west-central France. Valanjou isn't Valanjou anymore. In the year 2015 it merged with other communes. Chanzeaux, La Chapelle-Rousselin, Chemillé-Melay, Cossé-d'Anjou, La Jumelliére, Neuvy-en-Mauges, Sainte-Christine, Sainte-Georges-des-Gardes, Saint-Lézin, La-Salle-de-Vihiers, & La Tourlandry assimilated one with the others, along with Valanjou, to become Chemillé-en-Anjou, named for its principal seat of Chemillé-Melay. Such a principle, this division of things and peoples.

Prior to Bernier's visit to the Mogul Empire, geographers had divided the Earth according to its principal countries and regions. But he observed the World for himself; and he saw its many peoples; and while *all men differ in external form according to the different areas of the world in which they dwell*; and while *their features tend to be of such differentiated character* that One who Travels widely *can distinguish unerringly one nation from another*, despite these well known differences in physiognomy, through the wide errancy of his Travels Bernier conjectured *four or five Types of Races whose traits deviate to such a degree as to signal a departure toward a new Division of the Earth*. An experimentalist at heart. What stories must he have told the Khan in their hours of repose?

[Marginalia]

A twenty-first century philosopher named Davide Tarizzo said that the existence of race presupposes racism.

Historians and philosophers do not refer to Adolph Hitler as a German philosopher, perhaps because he did not love the truth.

Life is a big word with a lot meanings. NASA calls it the organic capacity to undergo Darwinian evolution. In retrospect, Tarizzo says, Darwin was a philosopher at heart, and he understood life as an inexhaustible force seeking to find and kill its carnal forms. The journey from one to the next could never possibly resolve itself. Lately, some people have said that there is no meaningful difference between the organism that lives and the machines it lives with. One modifies the other. Perhaps this cannot be resolved.

In many books I have read of gardens such as this one, Great Khan. Ancient gardens and new, gardens that will be built centuries hence, millennia, or in a future so distant their reality cannot be verified—gardens that reclaim the earth from men and grip his works with the hands of a universal sovereign. I have seen most of them with my own eyes, but few can match the splendor of yours. Not Cyrus the Great, ruler of the vast and powerful Achæmenid Empire; not Seleucus the First; not Soter, the first Ptolemy, that historian-savior of Alexander's people; none possess the riches of this, your earthly paradise. There is no language for my reverence of your boundless foundation of precious stones, the round fountain whose shape remakes the world in its entirety. Its glittering spray touches the very bottom of the heavens. The rushing water is the sound of the earth. Ships sail across its surface and wreck within its depths. The flowering stems and the verdant leaves, taller than any wilderness that has been recorded, must be home to every creature yet devised. It is a greater wonder than those mounds of rock the Egyptians use to deify their human rulers. I could traverse your paradise and never exhaust my eyes with the wonders to be found here. Could they be contained in any book? The gardens I have not seen, which are too many to name, I have only recently come across in texts: forgotten books that closed as soon as they were written, manuscripts that were left on shelves where they slept and gathered dust until finally, centuries later, they were taken down by some lover of esoteric knowledge. Let me, your humble physician, tell you of them, so that you may see what you already know with perfect clarity.

[Marginalia]

Welsh Indians are usually claimed to have descended from a colony founded by Prince Madoc in 1170 [Wikipedia].

In the September 5, 1805 entry of his journal, John Ordway speculated the Corps of Discovery had come across a band of Welsh Indians. He noted the strangeness of their language, inflected by some impediment or the vague presence of a brogue. Every word had to pass through half a dozen translations. He called these people the *likelyset and honestest Natives* the expedition had yet come across. He may have drawn this conclusion from a belief in the innate virtue of whites.

Frederick Jackson Turner said the frontier turned people into authentic Americans. Teddy Roosevelt said it was the slaughter of indigenous peoples, who were constitutionally unfit for democratic self-governance and had to necessarily succumb to the mighty tide of history. One might contest the desire for a first nation of European heritage.

Ordway's evidence is anecdotal and therefore impermissible as legitimate historical data.

A trifle bemused, he wrote of the difficulty of saying anything.

I could not tell if the book was real. No one had given it to me. I had found it beneath the bench of an Indian vessel during a voyage of two-and-twenty days toward Guendar. I was subsequently told that the river led to a great emptiness, that a metamorphosis happened little by little. Our watery route evacuated itself of all moisture, it became a river of sand. One drop turned to grain, another drop, another and another until all the water had become earth, and all the crew and passengers dissolved into luminous ambiences. I do not remember if it was me on that boat. I was immersed in the book I had found, lured into the gilded text and illustrations describing the gardens of Tamerlan, so celebrated for his conquests of the people of Great Tartary called the Mogols. I can read from it directly, slowly, word by word, from pages of the manuscript inscribed in my memory. There is a garden of voices that travel great distances. The voices travel here. The page here. The pages turn here. I do not know how to remember, or why I remember. It might not have been me. I might not remember anything. Within these glorious passages I see a map. Khan, you yourself, a luminous ambience. Great Khan. I have made my own version of this map. It is not correct. It is less incorrect than I have seen. It led me here. If you could see these passages for yourself. They might not be passages. They might be pieces. Pieces that return to me. I have never seen them. They might be points. Pieces that point. Here they are. Or that pass. This is that garden. Is it not?

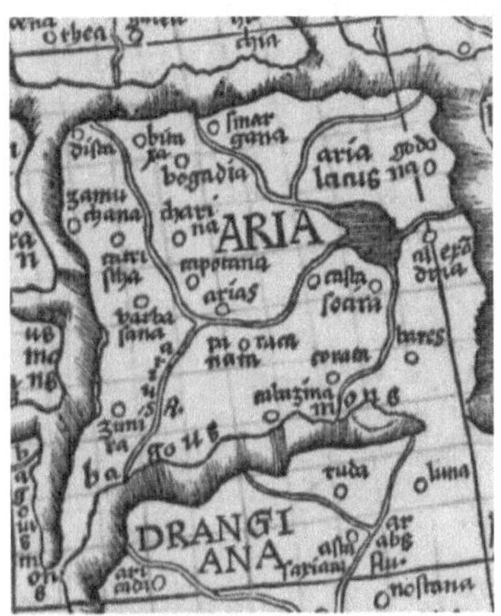

The farmer or engineer who cuts into the land can either cultivate it or devastate it.

Bernier, French [form of Aryan[needs citation]], included in the first Type all Europeans except for those born in Muscovy [i.e. Muscovite Rusi, Grand Duchy of Moscow, Tsardom of Russia, Russian Empire (Wikipedia)], as well as those from a small part of Africa ranging from Fez and Morocco, Algiers, Tunis, and Tripoli all the way to the Nile; included, too, was a large part of Asia, specifically the Empire of the Great Khan, possessor of the three Arabias, the whole of Persia [of which the seat was Yazd, the "City of Windcatchers," a reference to the natural ventilation systems common to traditional Iranian architecture; recognized by UNESCO as an historical city since CE 2017], the realms of the Great Mogul, of which the French physician [who posed often as a Greek] wrote extensively; the Kingdom of Golconda; of Bijapur; the Maldives; parts of the Kingdoms of Arakan, Pegu, Siam, Sumatra, Bantam, and Borneo. *For while the Egyptians, for instance, and the Indians are very dark, or rather sunburnt, this colouring is merely accidental for them, and results merely from the fact that they are exposed to the Sun—because those of them who protect themselves, and do not have to expose their skin as often as the Common People, are no darker than the Spaniards. It is true that most of the Indians are somewhat different from us in the shape of their faces and in a colouring that inclines them to the yellowish; but those traits do not seem to me enough to warrant classifying them as a separate type: or rather, if they were thus classified, you would have to create another special type for the Spaniards, and another for the Germans, and so on for all the peoples of Europe.* Like the Khan imagining his vast Empire, or the uncertain storyteller, Bernier could feel his system crumble as he was making it. Unfortunately for the Traveler, he had no sycophant to pacify him with wondrous tales. So he spoke.

[Marginalia]

Freud posited a concept called the death-instinct, which activated the innate compulsion of species to move from life to death. Natural selection, under this premise, does not necessarily select for life, by which the coordination of body and instinct of *each species is good for itself* [Darwin, the philosopher], but possibly death. What happens if history is an attenuation of drives rather than a struggle for their completion?

Racial categorizations in the United States have long been strictly assigned as a matter of heredity and descent, particularly along the rigid boundary separating black and white. This is the concept of the blood line, an outgrowth, in many ways, of the work of eighteenth century Natural Historians, themselves descendants, according to some social scientists, of François Bernier, a classificatory empiricist with a golden stylus. His division of human variety, they say, reconciled the individual to the immensity of the past, no longer explicable in terms of sin and redemption.

The same function Lukács gives to the novel centuries later. Perhaps the system of Types is the form of language offered to a broken world, perhaps it initiates the global breakage—the split *between what must live and what must die.*

I did not witness the garden of waves firsthand. Tavernier [have I not mentioned him?] whispered it to me as our caravan wended toward your kingdom. He was thirsty. He believed we were coming upon that seaboard once again in the middle of a vast desert. We had been wandering possibly for days or longer, possibly still we are on that voyage. Perhaps I merely imagine you, Great Khan, I speak to myself, or to no one. He was thirsty. When he opened his eyes again he saw a horizon of coastline, gigantic platforms fastened to the ground where sand and water mingled. *Tell me*, I demanded. I too was thirsty after years beneath the raging sunlight, and burned, chapped all over my hands and face. To move caused the stinging fissures of my skin to leak. Blisters pocked my face and ruptured the corners of my mouth. I tasted blood and the amber serums of infected tissue. My eyes were too dry to open. They blazed with the fire of the desert and the fire of the dying body. I was transitioning to a corpse. We were halfway there, to death and your city's walls. Our procession had dwindled somewhere, at some point, we had left a wake of dead and dying beasts as the rotting documents of our route. Spices spilled and swept, mixed with sand. Fabrics faded in the eternal high noon and dried to tatters. Horses, dromedaries, transients bleached and turned to dust. My words were empty breaths, breaths were vague contrails rising toward the heavens, my breathing was a parody of breathing. What could it sustain? *Tell me*, I whispered. *Tell me*. I saw what Tavernier saw, I saw an array of rafts tethered to a shoreline, rafts larger than any city, covered with fertile soil, bearing fathomless varieties of vegetables and trees, gardens rising and falling on the natural tides more lush and abundant than any found on dry land. Rising above the verdures were buildings of glass and stone, intricate machineries that transported materials and men from one point of a raft to another, and from raft to raft, from raft to sea and raft to land, connected to the water and the earth by mechanical passages across which trundled iron vessels billowing clouds of steam. For years, my eyes devoured the constant motion, the ebb and flow of the tide, the many constructions and demolitions that characterized the city. I inhaled those mechanized gusts of steam, they entered me, my body became both iron and flesh in that intermediate zone, I was entangled in the encounter, the coast, the breathing line of water and earth, the desert beneath.

[Marginalia]

Grave dowsing is considered by some archaeologists to be a legitimate and cost-effective alternative to geophysical methods like radar and magnetometer surveying. With the simple use of twigs, an entire cemetery of unmarked graves can be mapped virtually for free. In some cases the gender of the deceased can even be divined.

[Office of the State Archaeologist,
University of Iowa, Burials Program]

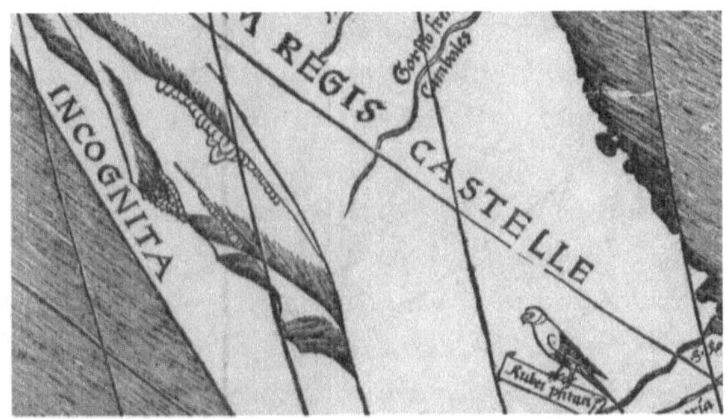

When one looks at the Indian cliff dwelling in Mesa Verde, one cannot separate art from nature. And one can't forget the Indian mounds in Ohio.

Bernier: *Among the second type, I place the whole of Africa, except for the Coastal areas just mentioned. The following features justify considering the Africans a distinct type: (i) their thick lips and their snub noses, for very few of them have aquiline noses and medium-sized lips (ii) the blackness that is their essential trait and whose cause is not, as people think, the heat of the Sun - for if you transport a Black man and a Black woman to a cold country, their children will continue to be black and so will all their descendants until they intermarry with white women. The explanation for their distinct type must therefore be sought in their sperm and their blood, both of which are, however, the same colour as in all the other types (iii) their skin is quite oily, supple and polished, except for the areas roasted by the Sun (iv) their beards consist of only three or four strands (v) their hair is not truly hair but instead a sort of wool similar to the coat of one of our hunting-spaniels and (vi) their teeth are whiter than the finest ivory and the whole inside of their mouths, like their lips, is red as Coral.*

Bernier, experimenter of boundaries and thresholds. Regarding his travels through the Mogul Empire, he claimed to provide simple amusement, an occasion *of relaxation from weighty affairs of State*, to Louis XIV. In telling of one thing, he wanted the warlike monarch to forget another. Was this his death drive? In seeking to fix his new division of human variety—in print, in speech, in thought—was he also, unconsciously, searching for a system that kills the increase of forms? Did he yearn for domination? Did he yearn for war? The traveling merchant, the king's physician, both Frenchman and artificial Greek (he passed, apparently). One can imagine him, immersed in his own alien report, straddling a coast everywhere he steps. A life both water and sand.

[Or, a different embedded figure, a different raconteur absorbed in the stories he tells. The Duke struts in, toweling his hair and sighing. He coughs three times, hacks, but doesn't spit. His robe seems a little strange at first, blue cashmere, cropped at his calves, belted with a sash of golden silk; he's just so spectacular in his plaid, his kerchief, his denim and gambler hat—here he is a notable sight removed from its accustomed trappings. His skin is tanned so deeply that one wonders whether it's residual from the autumn months, when he was filming *Big Jake* (1971) down in Durango and Zacatecas. He tosses the towel near a hamper in the corner by a mahogany bar, a veritable saloon behind which hang a row of gold-framed film posters (those of *The Alamo* and *True Grit* highest and centered), bottles glistening bronze and green (these catch the eye's peripheries and appear, momentarily, like fleets of Oscars). Even the light suggests a Western theme; the sun recedes beyond the Pacific so the Duke can take his place. He leaves behind him an open doorway looking out upon a rectangle of oceanside garden. Ferns spill from enormous clay bowls on short pedestals. A calm shimmer lilts palm fronds and, nearer the garden floor, primrose, honeysuckle, golden star, the taller flowers presiding sheriff-like over the lesser flora. Tips of spiraled topiary stand visible above the ridge where the garden slopes toward the water. Behind it all, a thin strip of ocean, the wide white side of an idle yacht. The Duke lights a cigarette, plunks down on the middle cushion of a wicker sofa. He crosses his legs, spreads arms wide across the cushioned back. He answers.]

WAYNE: *With a lot of blacks, there's quite a bit of resentment along with their dissent, and possibly rightfully so. But we can't all of a sudden get down on our knees and turn everything over to the leadership of the blacks. I believe in white supremacy until the blacks are educated to a point of responsibility. I don't believe in giving authority and positions of leadership and judgment to irresponsible people... The academic community has developed certain tests that determine whether the blacks are sufficiently equipped scholastically. But some blacks have tried to force the issue and enter college when they haven't passed the tests and don't have the requisite background...*

I wanted to create a truly realistic saddle bum of the West. I wanted to make him as honest and real as I could do it… I wanted… I wanted to…

Sam Peckinpah

[Marginalia]

Schopenhauer said that death is the *real result* of life.

It all begins with an unimaginably cold cloud [NASA]. Are stars capable of sustaining themselves through Darwinian evolution? Does the living organism contravene one half of its vital instincts? The anabolic rejection [cells assimilate, one to the other] of katabolic destruction [the breakdown of an order, the complex reduced to its simpler parts]—like hearing a crackling voice pass across the transom, insisting that its fragments of sound and syllable make perfect sense?

Some historians and sociologists have said the Modern spirit resists stagnation and solidity, because Modernity is all about breaking down the barbarity and superstition of the Middle Ages. Karl Marx said that Modernity was a matter of *melting the solids*, then forging new and better ones.

No conclusive argument has been put forth indicating whether we are still Modern, or if we have ever been, or if the *dead hand* of a barbaric past still works beneath our hi-tech shirt cuffs.

Certain strands of nostalgia for an imagined pre-modern world have been variously referred to as primitivism, retrotopianism [apocryphal and eccentric], fascism, and, in the context of the United States, pastoralism [simple & complex], & national romance.

Thirteen billion years: cold stasis; dust cloud collapses under gravitational force to protoplanetary disk; collisions, collisions; constant motion, interplanetary; orbital regularity of middle age [1 billion - 10 billion]; fuel dwindles, red gigantism; heat, the white glow of death resolves to empty cold.

Even God's perfect system will not survive.

Do not cry, Great Khan. Your deserts are real. Your paradise is real. I see them with my eyes. I speak them out loud. They are as substantial as you before me. Do not cry, but if you must, please know your tears are beautiful and immense. I see life in them. They recall to me delightful abodes along Tavernier's dreamy coast, where shores appear as in the mind of God, in their raw nature, but they are no longer natural, for they are changed by what surrounds them. Dense cities, powered eternally by the sea and moon, sprawl up and down the paradisaical skirts, mediating land and ocean, cities that are both dwellings and gateways to further reaches. This is the staging ground for a vast and abiding exodus into the fruitful interior—the most appealing garden that can be devised, an armory of latent powers, a paradise within reach; none surpass it, not even yours, Great Khan, the preface to it.

The third Type: portions of the Arakanese and Siamese kingdoms, portions of the islands of Sumatra and Borneo; Japan, Pegu, Tonkin, Cochin-China [Cochinchina is a region encompassing the southern third of current Vietnam whose principal city is Saigon. It was a French colony from 1862 to 1954. The Vietnam War, also known as the Second Indochina War, and in Vietnam as the Resistance War Against America or simply the American War, was a conflict in Vietnam, Laos, and Cambodia from 1 November 1955 to the fall of Saigon on 30 April 1975 (Wikipedia)], China, the strip of Tartary lying between China, the Ganges, and Muscovy; Usbekistan, Turkestan, Tashkent, a small part of Muscovy, and *The little Tartars and the Turkomans who live along the upper Euphrates near Aleppo* [major theater in the Syrian Civil War of the early twenty-first century; bombed by Russian and Syrian governmental forces *back to the stone age*, as American president George W. Bush threatened to do to the Pakistani government after the terrorist attacks on 11 September 2001 (commonly monumentalized as '9/11') if they did not support the American invasion of Afghanistan, i.e. home to descendants of Bernier's Moguls of the First Type].

The fourth Type is the Lapps [i.e. the Sami, Saami, or Sámi; Finno-Urgic people of portions of Scandinavia, esp. northern halves of Norway & Sweden; *Eurasian*]. Bernier only ever saw two of these *nasty creatures* in Danzig [i.e. Gdańsk], characterized by their *fat legs, big shoulders, short necks and faces somehow elongated, terrifying-looking, resembling a bear's*, these *nasty drinkers of fish-oil which they think better than all the nicest liquors in the world.* To supplement his scant personal experience, he studied pictures and second-hand accounts given to him by people who had visited the Country of the Lapps.

But what of these coast dwellers, these sea people, these watery folk whose essential traits bleed into uncertainty? Bernier does not speak of them in his New Division (not explicitly, at least). Instead, he turns to tales of beauty and sex. An aesthete of human formations.

[Selective Memory]

K. Pearson, social reformer, a eugenicist

America is one case in which we have to mark a masterful human progress following an inter-racial struggle. The struggle means suffering, intense suffering, while it is in progress; but that struggle and that suffering have been the stages by which the white man has reached his present stage of development, and they account for the fact that he no longer lives in caves and feeds on roots and nuts. This dependence of progress on the survival of the fitter race, terribly black as it may seem, gives the struggle for existence its redeeming features; it is the fiery crucible out of which comes the finer metal. You may hope for a time when the sword shall be turned into the ploughshare, when American and German and English [i.e. the myth of the continuously Teutonic] traders shall no longer compete in the markets of the world for their raw material and for their food supply, when the white man and the dark shall share the soil between them, and each till it as he lists. But, believe me, when that day comes, mankind will no longer progress; there will be nothing to check the fertility of the inferior stock; the relentless law of heredity will not be controlled and guided by natural selection. Man will stagnate.

What are the instruments of war? *What are
the essential and desirable traits? What should be
selected? What live, what die?*

An historian named Alexis de Tocqueville
believed that Modern history tended toward
equality. For a while he toured the United
States, writing of the things he saw. He said
that in the young nation everyone was equal,
and the equality of social conditions shaped
the nation's laws and institutions, and also the
habits of thought and deed practiced by every
citizen, down to their very ideas of the world.
Tocqueville saw the substances of a primordial
spirit, like a pond in eternal winter, hardening
into a nation that would endure the fluctuations
of time.

Nazi architect [& Minister of Armaments;
imprisoned after Nuremberg for his use of
forced labor in munitions factories] Albert
Speer imparted ruin into his designs. Nazis saw
their buildings as monuments to their political,
martial, and racial superiority. Their buildings
were to leave great ruins, as durable and pleasing
as those of Greece and Rome. Speer named this
implicit aspect of Nazi architecture *ruin value,*
the quality of triumphing in diminished form
after an encounter with genuine disappearance.
This was one response to what the Nazis called
Entartete Kunst. He explained his theory of
ruin in his prison memoirs, *Inside the Third
Reich.*

Tocqueville saw *majestic organization* in the North American continent's *extreme variation of scene.* He said the Mississippi basin *is the most magnificent habitation that God ever prepared for man.*

Speer once built a cathedral of light.

[Marginalia]

Birth and mortality rates, population control, demography, epidemiology, public health, disaster response, redlining, psychological operations [PSYOP], preparedness and prevention, performance optimization, market segmentation, the mass anticipation of terror——

Anthropologists have written about the piling up of history in the late twentieth and early twenty-first centuries. Because of ubiquitous recording technologies, such as smart phones, cell towers, state-run surveillance apparatus, private sector algorithms and web tracking infrastructure [e.g. Google, Facebook], cable and satellite TV, etc., an event is imbued with historical status as soon as it occurs; it is inscribed into a collective memory [most is not recorded, most is lost, most is rendered anecdotal and thus illegitimate], hardened into its monumental image [e.g. Flight 11 crashes into the north tower of the World Trade Center; first twin gashed, first to perish]. A desire emerges to evacuate time and space of all specificity and significance.

A twentieth century invention is the nuclear shadow. The ultraviolet radiation of atomic blasts can burn so intensely as to change the color of surfaces exposed to it; some objects, some animal and vegetable life forms, caught in the explosion leave behind an imprint upon being vaporized. This is their final image.

Nuclear shadows have to be photographed in order to remain for posterity, the flash always changes what it illuminates.

Two Frenchmen, two evacuated entities with no names no identities no bodies wrote of the concept war machine. The war machine is a *nomadic* process, constructed without any ready-made formal criteria. It emerges, dissolves space, turns to liquid again; one thinks of the Mongol hordes terrorizing the steppes. Perhaps the war machine is a need of map makers and map destroyers alike; not everyone wants to be removed from home, not everyone acknowledges the map.

† *Whoever's homeless now, will build no shelter; who lives alone will live indefinitely so, waking up to read a little, draft long letters, and, along the city's avenues, fitfully wander, when the wild leaves loosen.*

[Here, perhaps, the Duke gets up, wanders to the bar, where he snuffs his cigarette in an ash tray whittled from an elephant's tusk and selects a bottle drunk halfway down the label. Not sure how much time has passed, how long he has been speaking, for the printed words are in the last analysis a matter of editorial selection, a small sampling of what he's *actually said*—a sample stripped of the glimmer, stripped of the notable sight of *THE DUKE HIMSELF*, that is, *THE DUKE IN THE FLESH*. Certainly he pulls a cork with his teeth, spits it to the floor (who cares what happens to it), and tilts the bottle back. A straight talker, a straight shooter. The Duke fires words without aiming.]

WAYNE: *I don't feel we did wrong in taking this great country away from* [the Indians], *if that's what you're asking. Our so-called stealing of this country from them was just a matter of survival* [emphasis mine, E.B.]. *There were great numbers of people who needed new land, and the Indians were selfishly trying to keep it for themselves.*

A proposal of four or five Types of Race. In his paragraph on Americans, Bernier muses on the undecidability of the last. *They are really mostly olive skinned and their faces have a rather different shape from ours. Nevertheless I do not consider that that difference is so large as to warrant making them a special type distinct from our own.* Fifth type, subdivision of the first, evasion of the classificatory system. Type and not, solid and not, division marked with a faint and dotted line. For Bernier [for Tocqueville, for Turner, for Roosevelt, for preembodied Frenchmen, etc.], there is no reality to this ~~fifth~~ group. It is liquid running through his hands.

Perhaps he sought to freeze this ambiguity. Perhaps he sought to kill its spread. In his tales of traveling the Mogul Empire, Bernier describes Kashmir as such: *The first mountains which surround it, I mean those nearest to the plains, are of moderate height, of the freshest verdure, decked with trees and covered with pasture land, on which cows, sheeps, goats, horses, and every kind of cattle is seen to graze. Game of various species is in great plenty,—partridges, hares, antelopes, and those animals which yield musk. Bees are also in vast abundance; and what may be considered very extraordinary in the Indies, there are, with few or no exceptions, neither serpents, tigers, bears, nor lions. These mountains may indeed be characterised not only as innocuous, but as flowing in rich exuberance with milk and honey.*

Climbing the mountains, he briefly held the illusion that he was back in Auvergne [i.e. popular twenty-first century tourist destination in central France; name provisionally amended to Auvergne-Rhône-Alpes after territorial reform of French Regions in 2015, made official by Conseil d'État 28 September 2016 (Wikipedia); Auvergne-Rhône-Alpes is famous for its skiing and other outdoor recreational activities].

Bernier exhibits his powerful capacity for wonder when he re-imagines the world in front of him, seeing Europe where it has not yet staked its claim. The resemblance is uncanny, perhaps suggesting something in the blood of both regions. See the profuseness of European flowers. The ground is lacquered with them. *The whole kingdom wears the appearance of a fertile and highly cultivated garden.* A latent resemblance that only the delusional eyes of a traveling conqueror could glimpse—like Ordway, whose confusion led him to see Europeans where they could never be.

The Brussels Times, 16 September 2019 online English language edition:

> Asked by The Brussels Times if the situation in Kashmir has improved since India revoked its autonomous status, president Khan replied that, "Nothing has changed although India might want to give the impression that this is the case".

> "On the contrary, the situation has deteriorated even more. Thousands of people, including young teenagers, have been arrested, women are sexually harassed, houses are raided, streets deserted and shops and pharmacies have run out of stocks. The humanitarian crisis in Indian-controlled Kashmir is one of the worst in the world in recent years".

> "There are hundreds of thousands of Indian soldiers and police in Kashmir that have been given impunity to act against an unarmed civil population," he said.

> **Are India and Pakistan willing or capable to negotiate or do they need mediation via UN or EU?**

The September 11th terrorist attacks are a popular source of paranoid theorization. Some people believe American president George W. Bush was instrumental in planning the hijackings and collisions. Some believe the beams in the towers were planted with powerful ballistics, because jet fuel allegedly cannot melt steel. Some people who cannot sleep report turning on their radios late at night, when sound travels easily across broad distances. In 2016, a woman in a midwestern city sat up in her kitchen with a cup of tea, listening to a call-in talk show about supernatural events while thinking of her son, who had died on the same day as Johnny Cash. Beneath the laconic speech of the host, in the hissing silences between calls, she detected a pale crackling, the small sounds of exhalation. Upon turning up the volume, she deciphered whispers, broken words, the last messages of one victim from the north tower. It said a name. It said it missed its loved ones. It screamed.

Aside from legend, there is no documented evidence that Welsh Indians have ever existed.

[pages been lost somewhere; maybe shelved still inside a manuscript, maybe burned; maybe Bernier resumes his tale from some remote beginning; maybe he'd been on pause and begins again, mid-thought; this here is what's left, the remainder; maybe it's all he said, and the suggestion that more should exist confuses the Khan just as much as it does us; might be apocryphal; might not be Bernier at all, no one knows if, or to what extent, he may have authored it] * * * * *
* *

————was the hearth space of a new world, the greatest and most magnificent that could exist. And that's why it remains always displaced. It is a garden relegated both to past and future, to nature and machine, to neither, each claims a version of it, each claims the whole. There is no whole. It is a heterogenous nothing. I saw strange bodies there. I saw animals breathing steam, automatons laughing at the sweetness of oats. Is it possible to write something without knowing what you are writing? Is it possible to do anything else?

The Khan appears pacified, still something troubles him. The day's heat has lingered deep into evening. It is a vague warmth, a loitering exhalation of desert. He reclines, legs extending, they seem to increase in length the further back he lies. His weight transfers to an elbow, he sinks into the low couch under the deep shadow of a cypress tree. The darkness gathers like a flood and takes him, or perhaps he merely recedes. Only his folded hands, the linen concealing his legs, and his bare feet appear in full. His toes touch the Traveler, pressing into the meatiest part of his thigh. After some time a breeze lifts, disturbing the branches of the tree. For a moment the moonlight bleeds, and Bernier stares into the Khan's watering eyes. The ruler does not appear to breathe, nor to see what is plainly in front of him. His tears are of the same substance as the night. In the time it takes the Traveler to part his lips, the wind dies, and the night reclaims the teardrops. *It will all go away*, the Khan says.

Dusk is setting, but he ain't ready to go back yet. Out beyond the buttes, a golden-blood color that even now in late May reminds him of autumn in the Adirondacks. Every night, a final peace sets in here. His ride—a young quarter horse that still has a little of the wild prairie in him, that still champs at the bit—blows steam from its nostrils, grunting from hunger and fatigue, and for a moment he thinks of the fusillades on San Juan Hill and the idiocy of the legislators in regards to trade and commerce and of stroking the muscled flanks of Little Texas on the eve of battle, whispering messages of brotherhood and affection in that old beast's flickering ear, now long gone, a flickering that reiterates itself in the soft grasses rising and falling across the badlands, as if responding to the whispers he had breathed before the century turned. Feels that distance, hard and stony, like an impenetrable phalanx. That was all of a different age. Now he's here. The quarter horse wants to go back. It resists his pull. But he ain't ready yet. He might never be. Maybe it's the rhythm in the grasses that does it, or their contrast with the stoic aura of scoria and sandstone concretions, or maybe the vague sense that one day his name will be attached to this prodigious collection, and because of this it is his greatest creation, that he coerces the horse toward a flat enclave off the trail where it can pasture and he can subside for just a while longer.

He hobbles the animal and grabs some things out of the saddle bag and plods to a tree near the broad edge of the escarpment. The beast shakes its head and fusses. It whinnies once or twice and tries to rear. Eventually it notices the grass stomped flat under its hooves and sets to grazing.

He can only think to stare. He is looking at rock and scrub, peaks and dips, atmospheric traces of dust, the meniscus of sun dropping in the west.

The horse chews a mouthful of beaten grass. It dips its head and beetles its lips through weeds and grit in search of thicker sheaths. To his right, in the north, darkening thunderheads spark with lightning. Billowed contours appear in the intermittent flashes and linger on his retinas. Feels the lines of his face turn permanent and durable. Everyone stares at him.

The horse burrows its snout in the sand, raises its head and nods as if trying to shake something loose deep between its ears. Even in the golden-purple dimness he can make out the waving grass. Once this place was open abundance, a portal to the future. The wind is an encroachment, it is the death rattle of a wilting lung.

He would sup here on the victuals of the land. He would look to the quarter horse and share its wild itch. *I am like you*, he would say. *I will relinquish history and shed my human clothes and be your brother in creation. I will go with you.* He would enter the circle. He would repeat the primal form of all things living and nonliving. He would be time blowing across the buttes like a wind. It shreds the clouds and all the rains and yet the stone formations weather its gales like a fleet of angelic mastheads bracing for war.

He titters without knowing why. Everything is a reiteration of some prior thing. Everything is an antecedence. There is no end to it.

The moon rises and falls across the surface of his eye. The pince-nez hangs from its string and lightly swings. He sees. He opens his mouth and sees. Visions from the future infiltrate his nexus.

Once, when he was a young rough rider, still a tenderfoot, he wanted to kill a buffalo before they went extinct. Most that had been in Dakota were slaughtered by the Army and commercial hunters. Doesn't remember how many he put down. Fell one that was eight feet high at the shoulder. They became an American symbol because they nearly were exterminated from the face of the earth; they represented a world on the vanishing edge. Bones were tossed in winding piles like a lifeless cortex spreading across the earth.

He once believed the citizen was defined by his capacity to commit mass murder. He is obsessed with death. Beat back superstition and atavism, fill the world's waste spaces with light and motion. He would cry if he were someone else.

Here is his great legacy. The moon freezes in his pupil. The grasses shuffle. Behind him, the quarter horse grunts and whines. It wants sugar. Despite its feral restlessness, it wants to stable.

Behind him also, back there, are Chippendale settees, electric lamps, upholstered sleeping cars, silk vests, ruffled skirts, shoes fastened with laces and buckles elevated on wooden heels, buggies with curtains in the windows that rock on gentle springs like vessels coasting across calm waters, three story houses with wires in the walls and turrets on the roof, pipes that creak and fill entire rooms with warmth, streets cobbled with stones cut square, automobiles assembled part by part on moving belts and fueled by an ancient substance harvested from the earth more valuable than gold. All these encroachments. All these markers of progress. All these conquests of distance and time, conquests of death, these markers of a receding world.

Is he continuous? His Teutonic blood, his name fixed in ink? Was he always this? Shall he always be? Is he more or less than a processing center of linkages and interruptions? Extensions and cessations? This place where the romance of his life began, is this also where it will end? If he could retreat into the wide niche of this reserve. If he could melt into stone and soil. If he could run along its anchored borders. If the warrior could maim and kill himself and continue living as a result. If his blood crusade could flow and stop. If time could harden into something durable. If the earth could orbit nonetheless.

Khan. Sovereign. American. *It will*, he breathes… *It will all…* His hand moves. It attempts to seize the swaying flora in the pages of his field book. How does he make it permanent? How does he make it last against the coming onslaught, the future he created when he won the West, the future that is a repetition of the war he always wages? The leaves flicker in the wind. He tosses book and pen aside. He cannot vanquish wild motion with lines that bleed and dry.

RUIN

[1]

Miracle and wonder. Dig the range of the Possible at the end of the 20th Century, Folks! Consider that I am now in the Business Class cabin of Swissair Flight 122 plunging toward Europe when only yesterday morning I was creeping up a talus slope in southern Utah at a pace that took me 7 miles in the same time I will require tonight for the arc from Cincinnati to Zurich. We take these things too much for granted, I think.

There is a nearly full, though waning, moon off the starboard wing and we have just left what would be Maine were we not 35,000 feet above it. Where there is no place at all. "Here" in the stratosphere it is as uniform as Cyberspace and, as in Cyberspace, the only detail is within. I'm crossing a wide sweep of times zones, so time doesn't matter. And that irrelevance of such brief time is about the only present similarity to where I've been for the last week.

At first sunlight yesterday morning, I was in Another Time. I felt Neolithic as Og, living in a cave in the bottom of Utah's Dark Canyon, a fissure that forks like geological lightning through the cedar-speckled slickrock…

John Perry Barlow, "Barlow in Rockspace", Electronic Frontier Foundation [EFF], 1999

† Full of merit, yet poetically, man
Dwells on this earth.

[2]

Pancho and Itsumi, who he insists on calling Lefty, nose onto the Central Freeway in San Francisco's Mission District, ride the long curve through fields of warehouses, machine shops, storage units, and refurbished luxury apartments, and head toward the Bonneville Salt Flats 700 miles east. Pancho rides shotgun with a bare foot hanging out the window. Long ago, before he can remember, he gave up wearing shoes. The wind raises his awareness of the plantar and tibial zones, a resistance that cools and soothes across its vague and modulating pressure points. He sermonizes on the beauty of the false confession; on the future hybrid organic-synthetic virus that will invade humans through their electronic devices and drive us all to murder. He drinks cold one after cold one and tosses the empties out the window. He scans the internet for headlines. *Deadly Crash Snarls I-80 Traffic in Sacramento County* [KCRA. com]; *Fatal Crash Involving Big Rig, Motorcycle Closes Lanes on I-80 Near Antelope Road* [FOX40]; *Major Delays on I-80 as Jackknifed Tractor-Trailer, Fuel Spill Closes Multiple Lanes* [NJ.com]. Pancho and Itsumi are the two and only members the Paraboloid Microkingom. Itsumi believes the desert is a QR code waiting to be deciphered, a graveyard waiting to be revealed.

[3]

A triptych of works sold together: Smallpox, HIV, Untitled Future Mutation…

Of all human infectious diseases, smallpox is believed to have resulted in more human deaths throughout history than from any other single pathogen. The causative agent of smallpox, Variola virus, was eradicated from natural existence in 1977, through a global vaccination effort administered by the World Health Organization (WHO).

HIV represents the present. HIV/AIDS was first clinically observed in 1981 in the United States and although there is much medical research into the virus, currently, no cure exists.

A future virus that has yet to be born. Has this virus been created in the laboratory or evolved naturally? Will the impact of this virus be of benefit or hinderance to humanity?

Luke Jerram, from statement on "Glass Microbiology"

[4]

Aurelio Saavedra crosses the border at Tijuana in a 2008 Challenger, ochre like the color of the desert. The CBP agent takes off his aviators and stares into the big man's eyes. He might recognize Saavedra for his role on the 1973 Oakland Athletics, the second of three consecutive World Series championship teams. Even though he was a backup, he famously robbed Rusty Staub, Le Grande Orange, of a decisive three-run homer in the eighth inning of Game 1. More likely the CBP agent, an Anglo, is suspicious of all Mexicans who enter the United States or simply hates them outright. He asks if Saavedra has anything to declare.

No, sir, he says.

He perches his elbow on the window frame, yawns, and glances at his eyes in the rearview mirror, red and aching from consecutive nights awake and shot after shot of whiskey and tequila and whatever other liquor was at hand, interrupted every hour or two with the strongest coffee Anna and Alejandra could find in the cupboards of their tiny apartment and urge him to drink. The CBP agent calls his partner to Saavedra's car. The partner himself is Mexican or maybe Guatemalan. They ask him to open the trunk. Together they toss his suitcase and examine its contents. After several minutes they put back his clothes and toiletries and apologize for any inconvenience. The partner stamps his passport. He shows them his World Series ring. They welcome him back to the country where he became famous, if only somewhat, and if only for a year or two.

[5]

Rock Hudson was a Hollywood sex symbol who died of complications from the AIDS virus. The cause of his death shocked a base of fans and admirers who had not associated Rock Hudson with homosexuality, their assumption being that only homosexuals incurred and incubated HIV/AIDS. A teenage hemophiliac famously contracted the virus in 1985 after undergoing a blood transfusion. He was not allowed to return to school after his diagnosis and died in 1990, following a long and arduous legal battle that mirrored the battle for his health. Concerned citizens panicked over the possibility of an unhygienic population; they feared one could become infected by breathing, or the incidental transfer of bodily fluids like sweat or saliva. Don DeLillo's 1985 novel, *White Noise*, famously depicts scenes of an airborne toxic event. Amanda Blake was the actress who played Miss Kitty in 569 episodes of the TV Western, *Gunsmoke*. Blake died in 1989. The official cause of her death was cardio-pulmonary arrest due to liver failure and CMV hepatitis, rumored to have been triggered by the AIDS virus which she may have received from her womanizing husband. Theories continue to exist, stating the United States government possesses a cure for HIV/AIDS, which they deliberately withhold from the public for political, military, and commercial reasons.

[6]

If there had been no railway to conquer distances, my child would never have left his native town and I should need no telephone to hear his voice…

Sigmund Freud

[7]

Saavedra rolls into the parking lot of an apartment complex one block from the beach. He drops his duffel bag by the door, strides directly to the refrigerator, and pulls out a bottle of Mexican Coca-Cola. The balcony of the fourth floor unit overlooks La Jolla Cove and part of the complex's parking lot. From his wicker chair, the roof of the Challenger is visible between a Ford pickup and a Toyota Corolla. He sips the fizzy soda and watches people arrive and depart from the complex for a little while before turning his attention to the cove. Families come and go in no particular pattern or rhythm. Eventually his gaze settles on two children pounding toy hammers in the surf. They seem to be playing archaeologist, freeing seashells embedded in the rocks. They strike with great care, as if saving a victim from smoldering wreckage, or excising pieces of garbage that have fused with the mineral structures of the coast. Tiny woodsmen, he thinks, small enchanted lunatics, what tunes they might whistle day and night. After the sun sets, he goes down to the outdoor shopping center across the street and eats at the bar of a seafood restaurant specializing in baskets of battered shrimp. He orders a steak and lobster tail and a liter of Tecate. The bartender asks about his World Series ring. He tells her the story. Afterward, he walks around the shopping center for half an hour to aid his digestion and, probably, enjoy the simple pleasure of being among people who appear carefree and content and unaware of their surroundings. On a whim he enters a souvenir shop and after sifting through racks of knick knacks and clothing, purchases a t-shirt printed with the movie poster for *The Outlaw Josey Wales*, which he slips over his polo shirt. He walks along the beach to the apartment, gazing at the moon and its reflection fanning out across the Pacific.

Lying in bed, he reads a chapter from a book called *Arcadia/Remains* by the American novelist Arnold Koch. His sleep is deep and luxurious and filled with astonishing dreams. He sees two women racing horses across the pastures of a secluded ranch in Sonora or Chihuahua. The mountains surrounding the grassy valley extend to the outer edges of the solar system. On the other side, the infinite world is on fire. The screams of the annihilated transform into wind and birdsong. The mountains emit the warmth of Hell that the racing women, whose horses are huge and beautiful and never tire, mistake for the warmth of the sun. They do not know what time is even though it bears down upon them. They raise their faces to the sky. The sweat on their foreheads glimmers. Like always he forgets the dream upon waking even as it registers in his elevated pulse and the wide diameter of his pupils and his rapid breaths. At first he does not know where he is. He drinks another Mexican Coke on the balcony and stares across the ocean, glancing at *Arcadia/Remains* now and then. Light from the east slowly bleeds across the surface. He thinks vaguely of Christ walking over the Sea of Galilee. After showering, toweling himself dry, and dressing in the previous day's blue jeans and the Josey Wales t-shirt, he goes into the bedroom and opens the closet, where a steel safe is concealed behind a stack of obsolete printers and computer monitors. He gets down on his knees and pulls a scrap of paper from his pocket and spins the tumbler according to the combination someone had written for him. He opens the door, and as he had been promised, there is the big one, resting on a small strip of purple velvet among several stacks of hundred dollar notes and three boxes of ammunition, the gold-plated .50 calibre Israeli Desert Eagle. He holds it with both palms in a reverential semi-trance. Eventually, after a timeless interval of nothing, he puts the firearm and ammo in the duffel bag and leaves without locking the apartment. As he fills the Challenger at a nearby gas station, he decides it would be more pleasant to catch Route 1 at Dana Point and take it all the way up the coast to Alameda County, the scenic path of forests and cliffs and the great Pacific, far more pleasurable and, he must admit, cinematic than dealing with Disneyland traffic and, further north, the monotonous stretches of farmland that would brutalize him and cause him to silently weep if he went up Interstate 5.

[8]

In *Frankenstein; Or, the Modern Prometheus,* Mary Shelley speculated about the way in which our own creations might ultimately turn against us. In this nineteenth-century science-fiction fantasy, she challenged a modern notion of scientific progress by illuminating its darker side. In the twentieth century, novelist Arthur C. Clarke and film director Stanley Kubrick conceptualized a similar catastrophe. In *2001: A Space Odyssey,* the robot Hal eventually becomes paranoid and fearful of the humans who created him. He then uses his intelligence to destroy them one by one.

Many years ago, I was struck by a mural in the Bay Area that illuminates the concept of *ruins in reverse.* It depicted an abandoned San Francisco expressway where there were no cars and no humans; instead the expressway was crowded with endangered species. Mountain lions, buffalo, moose, and other soon-to-be-lost creatures that once roamed across the American plains now roamed across a barren highway that overlooked an urban landscape gone to seed, the world as we've known it, but ghostly, with no trace of human life. It was a view of contemporary civilization after our demise, when a catastrophic event, or a series of less obvious events, has created an inconceivable, mostly unimaginable time of life on a posthuman planet.

Carol Becker, "The Agitated Now," *PAJ: A Journal of Performance and Art,* 41.2, May 2019

[9]

Rosa and Johnny met in Las Vegas when she was still working as a waitress at the Aztec Club on East Flamingo Road. Johnny came in one night and drank at least five whiskeys with Mexican Coke, setting dollar after dollar on the stage. Every half hour he would raise his hand and call her over. She'd sweep by and place a new drink in front of him and he'd tip her a few bucks. Halfway through the night, he told Rosa she could see his badge. He was a lawman, he said, searching for someone. A woman not unlike her had gone missing from a similar place in Carson City. He had come down to Vegas to check whether she'd turn up in any clubs, which was usually the case. She hadn't seen anyone like that, not that she knew of, at least. The girls at the Aztec Club were local or undocumented or came from California on the weekends. She wasn't supposed to sit on the lounge floor during her break, she said, especially not with a customer. They moved to the end of the bar, a shadowy threshold separating the lounge from the offices and dressing room in back. They talked about some things before settling into a far reaching contentment, letting the colored lights roll across them in silence. They watched and listened as the mic jockey called out the next girl's name, and she slid and turned across the glassy stage to the steady pulses of "I Hate Myself for Loving You" by Joan Jett and the Blackhearts.

Five or six days later Rosa and Johnny were married. It's like we're living in a TV show, she said. I know, he said. It really is. I've never been so happy. They drove from Carson City to Vegas and back every weekend. They agreed that it felt like they lived in the desert, on the highway, in his cruiser. They were residents of the dust and scrub.

I suppose I'd just go out there and rot, he said, indicating the horizon beyond the windshield, when Rosa asked during one of these drives what he would ever do without her. I'd buy an acre and die there alone, and it would only cost me a dollar a month in property taxes.

[10]

The precise number of deaths in the Hiroshima and Nagasaki nuclear attacks is impossible to pinpoint. Part of the problem is that people keep dying, year after year, from leukemia and other fatal diseases associated with radiation poisoning. Another is the lack of documentation numbering the Chinese and Korean prisoners of war kept in Hiroshima as a forced labor reserve. Eventually, all of the initial survivors will run out. Fears of nuclear annihilation returned to the American consciousness after the 9/11 terrorist attacks; it is perhaps more accurate to say these fears were reactivated. Leucippus and Epicurus were atomists, because they believed the universe is made of indivisible parts, that many other universes are probable, that ours is an accident that occurred by the chance ordering of unpredictable cohesions. Some atomists believed that species were similarly accidental. Body parts once drifted freely in the ether, joining as they met, thus forming a pandemonium of creatures that were not viable, because their parts did not conduce the ultimate function of survival. The life forms that happened to result in harmonious functionality were the ones to survive and propagate. This is referred to as a microcosmic view of life, because individuals manifest the laws of the totality. Democritus believed the first humans were foragers who consumed the most convenient herbs and grasses, and their fear of wild animals drove them to associate with one another in prototypes of civil existence. Anaxagoras believed celestial bodies are hot stones. His name translates approximately to *lord of assembly*.

[11]

Saavedra drives up the coast with the .50 calibre Israeli Desert Eagle in his lap. He does not know whether he speeds like a maniac or coasts like he is stoned. The ocean sparkles, at some point when he turns his gaze west it is a looming abyss. It occurs to him he might not be on the same highway as he was earlier, he might have crossed into a different region, a region of walls and infinite depth, something vast and powerful might have played an evil trick on him. He stays the night at the place he owns in San Leandro, a split-level ranch house in a middle class neighborhood with a backyard and a covered patio, where he sits drinking shots of Mezcal until two or three in the morning, speaking intermittently to himself until he reaches the bottom of the bottle and finally consumes the worm. Lying awake, he observes out loud that the Josey Wales shirt is beginning to stink. He reaches for the phone on the nightstand and says some things to the private investigator, that macabre little fucker taking his place in Tecate.

[12]

Where do the roots of the mistake lie? Actually, they lie in Darwin's own words, which surreptitiously introduce a principle of utility, where one should instead talk of a *principle of vitality*. This is the sole and exclusive principle for selection: not the useful, but the vital. Variations are either for life or for death. And this is all natural selection sees. Therefore, there is no need to speak of utility. All that natural selection needs, in order to be operative, is to keep on choosing, to keep on selecting. Natural selection, in this sense, is the act of a will. But this will, anonymous and impersonal, is never combined with the comprehension of a purpose: the useful. Rather, it is nailed to its condition of possibility: vitality.

Davide Tarizzo

[13]

Johnny thought often, one might say obsessively, of that moment in the car when Rosa had asked the question that had seemed impossible to answer, what would he do without her—a question that must have come from a vague and speculative world that could only exist in a work of science fiction, which means she must have been a secret lunatic or a magnetized pole, gathering and passing messages from alternate realities or the nightmares people shed and forget upon waking. He recalled the sound of her voice, which now registered in his pulse and the nervous tingling emanating from his fingertips, he was a receiver transmitting signals from the dead. He could only compare her whispers to the wind or the infrequent rippling of the water in the irrigation canal marking the edge of his desert property, a small half-sound that sometimes carried in the evening breeze. He sat in the front seat of his cruiser every night, parked beside the chrome trailer shaped like the capsule of a giant antiretroviral, gazing toward the highway barely visible beyond the lot he had purchased with the small insurance payout after Rosa had passed away. He spent the rest of his time driving up and down U.S. Highway 50 with his radar gun turned on, listening for voices to pass through the static of his scanner. Once in a while he thought he heard a whisper or part of his name, after which he would fix his stare on the road, pulling over daredevils who screamed like meteors across the Great Basin. He warned them one by one of the dangers they might face if they did not slow down. Once or twice a driver commented to the woman riding beside him that the cop who ticketed them seemed half alive, as if he had been trapped for millions of years in a glacier and was just recently thawed, or worse, like he had been in the process of dying but stopped halfway through.

[14]

The men of the New Republic will rout out and eliminate urban rookeries and all places where the base can drift to multiply; they will contrive a land legislation that will keep the black, or yellow, or mean-white squatter on the move;… so that childbearing will cease to be a hopeful speculation for the unemployed poor;… This thing, this euthanasia of the weak and sensual, is possible. On the principles that will probably animate the predominate classes of the new time, it will be permissible, and I have little or no doubt that in the future it will be planned and achieved.

H.G. Wells, self-proclaimed futurist, the "Shakespeare of science fiction" [qtd. Aldiss]

[15]

Saavedra arrives in Tahoe after sunset. He eats dinner in the restaurant of a ski lodge on the northwest shore of the lake and spends part of the night in a room on the fourth and topmost floor. As far as he can tell, he is the only guest in the entire building. Around 11:00 he gets out of bed, rinses himself in the shower, and heads down to the bar wearing his Josey Wales t-shirt and blue jeans with the Israeli Desert Eagle tucked in the waistband. For an hour he leans against the bar, the only patron, this being July and the height of the offseason. Nonetheless, the bartender says, the resort stays open year round. There is no shortage of hikers and campers, people who drive up from San Francisco to reconnect with mother nature. The problem, he says, is that they take San Francisco with them, the traffic and the stress on municipal systems, like the sewers and hospitals and broadband networks. From the moment the first real estate developer saw an opportunity to make Tahoe a vacationer's destination, everything slowed down, and the obstructions have only piled up since. In fact, he says, Tahoe is made of obstructions. There would be no Tahoe if the gridlock didn't bring it into existence. The weekend rushes, the rates of resource consumption, the marketing materials. That's Tahoe.

So this is an illusion, Saavedra says, indicating the empty bar.

Yes, the bartender says, this is an illusion. That's it exactly. Everything that happens lingers here like a ghost and prefigures the next event. Next week there's a convention of twenty-first century adventurers staying on the second and third floors. They're all from San Francisco, I'm sure of it. Some of them might be billionaires. They bring their apps and drones and tech crews, a bunch of people that function as their retinues, and use them to document their hikes, which aren't real hikes since they go up and down the trails that are already well worn and sometimes paved. They're only interested in taking pictures of themselves, I think. They don't want to chronicle their experiences so much as make new ones that can only exist on the internet.

A little later the bartender stops charging Saavedra and puts the bottle of rye he'd been pouring from on the counter. He prepares an Old Fashioned for each of them and tells the story of an urban hiking club that allegedly found and killed a hermit living in a cave in the Sierra Nevada. They took turns posing with him for photos, because he had a long beard and was dressed in rags, including the one tied around his head. This was shortly after 9/11. They wanted pictures because they thought he looked like bin Laden. They joked they'd found the notorious international fugitive and he'd been hiding right under George Bush's nose. Their hike, which had originally been meant to connect the group to an earlier and probably imaginary time when humans lived happily among trees and sunshine, turned into an unexpected photo-op. They rounded a switchback, and there in a crevasse was this unwitting impersonator of the most famous terrorist to ever live. First they photographed each other shaking hands with him, then trying on some of his rags, then posing him in different positions they found humorous, then putting a rag over his eyes, then bending him forward and pretending to sodomize him with a fallen tree branch, then tying more rags around his face and binding his wrists with rope, then pulling down his pants and doing the same with his ankles, then spanking him on his ass with the branch, then pushing him over, then shoving a fistful of leaves in his mouth, then pretending to kick his ribs, then actually kicking him, then pretending to piss on his face and actually pissing on him, then squatting around him as if he was a buffalo one of them had felled with a rifle, then etching marks like swastikas and satanic numerals into his arms and legs with a pocket knife, then, then, then… It was a terrifying reenactment of Abu Ghraib. I know all this because he was my father's brother. He went up into the mountains to live a life of peace and meditation, and had more or less succeeded for almost thirty-five years. My father thought it was a crazy idea when his brother first made the decision to withdraw right after the Tet Offensive, when his draft number was called on the evening news. Even by then, back at the dawn of Aquarius, tourism was a powerful reality. There was no place a person could go to live an untouched life. And yet he succeeded. My uncle probably didn't even know that 9/11 had happened. His death was a ripple effect of that famous breach of national security. And that's how things happen, they ripple from some prior source. I'm writing a book about subliminal social forces. Freud's double nephew was one of the fathers of advertising, you know. He was the one who got women to smoke. He called cigarettes Liberty Torches, so every woman with a cigarette in her mouth I suppose was like the Statue of Liberty. The Nazis made films of happy Jews building birdhouses and sweeping the streets of phony villages they forced the Jews to build for the pleasure of Red Cross inspectors. Of course the Nazis made their forced labor reserve tear down these happy scenes after the inspectors had left the ghettos and extermination camps. The Soviets, too. They had a whole program studying the methods and mechanics of magic and the paranormal. They wanted a whole army of warlocks.

Crazy stuff, Saavedra says, though he had stopped listening and had begun to ponder the ripples oscillating through his own life. He asks if the kitchen is open, then drives around the town looking for a late night eatery, venturing outside city limits, up into the foothills, around the shore, making his way into Nevada, where finally a 24-hour diner appears in the glistening fog of streetlamps. The building is small and vaguely tubular. Shit, he thinks, it's the bomb from *Dr. Strangelove*. He sits at a booth looking out to the parking lot. The Challenger is one of three cars, the others being a Pontiac Grand Prix and a Ford pickup emblazoned with the logo and telephone number of a local heating and cooling business. The heating and cooling technician sits at the counter drinking coffee, reading a mass market paperback called *Earthworks*. Saavedra places his order, a coffee and three scrambled eggs and a tall stack of pancakes. He eats and drinks in silence, skimming several passages of *Arcadia/ Remains*. Mostly he observes the dining room. Photos and paintings hang all over the walls, images of the Donner Pass and 19th century prospectors posed with their equipment at the mouths of bustling gold mines. There are also many pieces of Olympic memorabilia from the 1960 games, a couple of American and Soviet hockey jerseys and sets of ice skates and a pair of skis mounted in a St. Andrew's Cross above the door to the kitchen. The waitress looks out beneath this profanity every few minutes. Every time, a man's voice bellows through the threshold of the swinging door, a cyclops, Saavedra thinks, demanding milk. He is almost finished with his coffee when a young man dressed like a punk rocker saunters from the back hall leading to the bathroom. The boy drops some cash on the table and leaves, gets in the Grand Prix, and disappears along the winding road.

Around 2:00, half an hour after the heating and cooling technician has said goodbye to the staff and left, a police cruiser parks next to the single handicap spot. Two cops get out, one young and one old, maybe a rookie and a vet on the cusp of retirement, both with gloomy expressions as if they have just come from a murder scene, or that might simply be the faces of cops. The older one takes the seat of the heating and cooling guy. The youth plunks down on the stool beside him. Without asking, the waitress brings out two cups, a carafe, a bowl of creamer packets, a bottle of ketchup, and two servings of ham and hash browns. A few minutes later a Honda CR-V carrying two lovers in expensive Scandinavian sweaters pulls up. They stroll arm in arm into the diner and sit in a booth on the far wall, perpendicular to the front windows, beneath a framed photograph of the Olympic hockey team. They tap on their phones intermittently and order two coffees and a single bowl of fruit. While waiting, they play some sort of game where one suddenly takes the other's picture, and the one whose picture is being taken pretends they do not wish to be photographed.

The young man, really a boy, is Germanic looking and tall. His hands are wide with long fingers and his broad shoulders have not yet filled in. He might have come here directly from the Crimean front. The woman or girl is Mexican, maybe sixteen or seventeen years old with hair down to her waist and golden hoops in her ears and bright red lipstick expertly applied. Her hands are small and delicate, at least that's how they appear to Saavedra, as if she had always just dropped something, the grip of her guardian, or they had remained the hands of a little girl while the rest of her grew up around them. Her laugh is nearly inaudible, yet it dominates the room, it is the single phenomena Saavedra can perceive at certain moments, when he sets down his cup or wipes the corners of his mouth.

He studies the lovers for the duration of their feast, he eavesdrops on the patrolmen, their utensils slice through the ham and bring it to their salivating mouths in pieces.

What if the life of one person can pause while the life of another continues at full speed? What if, due to the laws of relativity and particle physics, two people can inhabit time on separate and simultaneous planes, like two characters stuck on different television channels?

[16]

It seems probable to me that God in the beginning formed
matter into solid, massy, hard, impenetrable movable particles,
of such sizes and figures and with such other properties and
in such proportion in space, as most conduced to the end for
which he formed them.

Sir Isaac Newton

[Addendum]

I saw a hare, & I beleve he run into a hole, he run on a hill &
disapeared, I Saw on this hill several holes.

William Clark

[17]

Saavedra re-enters the diner. He takes his old place in the booth at the window. The young cop glances at him and turns back to the old cop, who is in the middle of a story. After a few minutes Saavedra gets up and sits at the counter next to them. They study him and ask about his World Series ring. He tells them about it. That's great, they say.

I think I remember you, the older cop says. I've been in Carson City since 1971. I used to park at the edge of the lake sometimes and listen to the broadcasts. They'd come in clearer at night.

They ask about his t-shirt.

I was in San Diego for a few days. I went shopping. I don't know, it was an impulse. Then I drove up here for some reason. Well, not just any reason. Not for no reason at all. I'm looking for my daughter. I heard you talking about your wife and thought I'd take a seat. Can I buy you a coffee? Waitress, can I please get a coffee for these men? And one for me. Let's make that a trio of coffees.

Saavedra and the cops exchange names. The young one is called Carson, possibly his first or last name, or maybe a nickname based on the nearby city. The older one is called Johnny. He orders another serving of ham and tells the waitress he'll pay for it himself.

The Dodgers won it all in 1981, Saavedra says. All winter it was Fernando Valenzuela this, Fernando Valenzuela that. He's Sonoran, so he was a local boy doing good. My daughter left or was taken in December of that year. I don't know what one thing has to do with the other. I come up every so often and search. How would I even recognize her? I'm terrified that she has been dead for years and I won't get satisfaction.

Kind of like Josey Wales, says Johnny.

Kind of like Josey Wales, says Saavedra. That's exactly right.

Saavedra picks up the tab and agrees to follow the cops toward Johnny's trailer in the desert. Along the way, Johnny drops Carson at a reservoir, where a different cruiser is parked at the water's edge. Carson gets in, and suddenly he is very far away. Saavedra stares at the tail lights leading him through the darkened forest. They come to resemble two points stuck in the eternal dance of attraction and repulsion. They never quite cohere, never fully separate. He loses track of the turns, inclines, and declines as he makes his way. Shadows encroach on every side, they resemble a night within night, a time that has nothing to do with orbits and tides. He might not be moving, he might be stuck in an endless valley.

Back in the diner, Johnny had promised plenty of whiskey and a sympathetic ear. In a way, he said, he was committed to his own search, only his wife had not gone missing. She had died of AIDS complications in the late 80's, and he had come to learn that the task of his life is to find her in places he does not expect. He told Saavedra that no one should ever want to know, let alone find out, what happens when the lungs become like sponges submerged in a bucket of water. On occasion he has seen portions of her face very late at night in the static of his television, after a twitch in his muscles or a sudden emanation wakes him, sometimes when a storm rolls through or if the receiver goes off-kilter or if he feels an alien presence in his room. He sees the shape of her shoulder when his mouth goes dry and a breeze roils the curtains above his bathroom sink. He hears fragments of her voice when he sits awake, a zombie or half a corpse, absorbing the sounds of the scanner. He said this is what the fourth dimension must be like.

At some point during this endless wandering Saavedra observes that his foot has pressed the gas pedal to the floor.

He glances at the Israeli Desert Eagle resting on the passenger seat beside the Koch novel. It catches a passing headlight or the first glint of sun. He drives onward, possibly to the west, possibly into the forest or desert or the outer galaxy—a meteor with no trace.

[18]

If traveling across the ocean by ship had not been introduced,
my friend would not have embarked on his sea voyage and I
should not need a cable to relieve my anxiety about him.

Freud [cont.]

[19]

I wanted to create... I wanted to make him... I wanted... I wanted to...

197

Sam Peckinpah

[20]

Itsumi and her husband, Brad, take the number nine train from their apartment on the Upper West Side all the way to the Cortlandt Street Station. They walk a block to One World Trade Center, where her company, the Dai-Ichi Kangyo Trust Company of New York, is three months into a two year lease of the forty-eighth through fiftieth floors. His company, Marsh & McClennan, occupy what DOD, ATF, CIA, FBI, FEMA, and NSA forensics experts call the *impact zone*, floors ninety-three through ninety-nine. They scan their key cards, admitting access to the express elevator across the lobby from the security desk and the row of international flags displayed along the balcony façade, symbolizing the prowess of global capitalism at the end of history. He answers his cellular phone as the doors slide closed. In the moment before they seal, Itsumi catches a glimpse of the sky through the high arches of the lobby windows. Finally some sun and warmth. It has been storming for the last couple weeks with Hurricane Erin churning over the Atlantic. She might go for a run if Brad has to stay late [sounds like he might]. The elevator lifts. She puts a minute bend in her knees to prevent them from locking when it stops. After two minutes the doors open to the forty-fourth floor. They step out of the large express elevator into the sky lobby and board a smaller local elevator that stops at the forty-ninth floor. Itsumi and Brad kiss briefly and she squeezes her way out. A stack of paper rests on her desk awaiting signatures. As she steers among rows of cubicles, she detects the tiny, constant arcs of the swaying tower, always delightful and a little unnerving when she feels them; they are nearly imperceptible. The wind blows briskly from north to south.

The concept of the single-person corporation emerged sometime during the late twentieth century. It is impossible to pinpoint a precise origin. It did not appear as something thrown from the sea, but as the swell of the tide itself. The term may refer to multiple business arrangements. From the perspective of law and regulation, a person may incorporate an entrepreneurial enterprise of which they are the only human member in order to protect their private assets against litigation and loss. As a category of being [i.e. an *ontology* only possible under specific circumstances of history and culture], the term designates the increasing fragmentation of workers due to the twin forces of neoliberalism and globalization. The single-person corporation is a nomad figure, in some instances self-serving, following the flows of capital and prestige to where they are abundant, as the cowpunchers and gauchos of yore would guide their herds to slaughter; more commonly, this person is continually displaced, characterized by their fundamental, extrinsic traits of precarity and uncertainty. The freelancer, the farcical knight, the movable campaign.

Itsumi is an American by birth. Her parents emigrated from Kyoto in the 1960s. They watched the Apollo moon landing on television. She met Brad in Hiroshima in 1995, when they were both doing internships for their universities' global business programs. They were not sure how to behave during the city's commemoration of the American nuclear attack. The young Americans could not imagine the searing brightness splitting the horizon, the irradiated city blown to ash and lingering in the morning air… The same feeling of implosion characterizes her life for several years after Brad disintegrates in the astonishing heat of burning jet fuel and melting steel—unnamable, unspeakable, a modulating border zone splicing and sundering desolation, total misery, and the warped consciousness of disbelief.

[21]

In 1967 Robert Smithson wrote an essay for *Artforum* called "A Tour of the Monuments of Passaic, New Jersey," in which he narrated a walk along the banks of the Passaic River through his hometown. A portion of his journey spanned the construction site of a new state highway. Of the machinery, raw materials, and their arrangement in space, he concluded: *That zero panorama seemed to contain* ruins in reverse, *that is—all the new construction that would eventually be built. This is the opposite of the "romantic ruin" because the buildings don't fall into ruin after they are built but rather rise as ruins before they are built. This anti-romantic mise-en-scene suggests the discredited idea of time and many other "out of date" things.* Herodotus spoke of the out of date things he had seen in his own travels; the *salty extrusions that corrode even the pyramids*; the *blackish and clod-filled* Egyptian soil, far different from the red Libyan sands and Arabian clays, that appeared as if they had been carried far inland by a river; seashells high on the sides of mountains. Somewhere, Smithson eventually writes that the island of Manhattan contains within itself a natural desert—paved over, worked beyond visibility.

[22]

The phrase "ground zero" originates with the Trinity test [the original nuclear detonation, the harnessing of the power of the sun, cf. Harry Truman] in the Jornada del Muerto outside the town of Socorro, New Mexico. Socorro exists along a forgotten stretch of the Rio Grande. It is said to have been named in the sixteenth century by Spanish soldiers who emerged from the desert, dehydrated and on the brink of starvation. The detonation site is a registered historical landmark and is open to visitors. People with cameras gather around a commemorative obelisk that casts its shadow on the otherwise empty pan. An informational plaque at ground zero reassures visitors that *many places on Earth are naturally more radioactive than the Trinity Site.* Pat Garret shot Billy the Kid 176 miles east. It is a 57 hour trip from the Trinity Site to Fort Sumner by foot [Google Maps]. People are referred to as *downwinders* when the prevailing air currents carry radioactive fallout from nuclear tests to their homes. The desert outside Socorro is named, approximately, Journey of the Dead Man.

In the twenty-first century, the phrase "ground zero" often refers specifically to the site of the demolished World Trade Center in Manhattan's famed Financial District. Many first responders are dead and dying as a result of poisonous air. Seconds after impact, many toxic building materials comminuted and dispersed into the atmosphere. *As of December 2017, the most common conditions certified by the World Trade Center Health Program were rhinosinusitis, gastroesophageal reflux disease (GERD), asthma, sleep apnea, cancer, posttraumatic stress disorder, respiratory disease, chronic obstructive pulmonary disease, and anxiety disorder* [Wikipedia]. Some who have gotten sick in the intervening years believe their cancers are related to 9/11, but they cannot offer proof.

A garden of concentric circles marks the hypocenter of the Fat Man implosion-bomb detonated on 9 August 1945 over the city of Nagasaki, Nagasaki Prefecture, Japan. A black column rises solemnly in the center.

If you were to line up the individual pieces of rubble from the World Trade Center, the Pentagon, and the hijacked aircrafts in a horizontal line, they would span the continental United States for 2,666 miles. Many debris are housed in the 9/11 Tribute Museum. Many are lost to history. Some, it is speculated, have reemerged in new forms.

[23]

Itsumi drifts from one routine to another. She avoids the streets, the columns of sky and shadow produced by the variations of height that make the city, taking the subway at every opportunity instead until the London Tube is bombed on 7 July 2005 [i.e. 7/7] and she is forced back to the surface by this new specter of subterranean terror. She would maybe fly if it was a realistic possibility. Her contract expires at Dai-Ichi Kangyo seven months after the attack, one of which she spends with her mother in Berkeley. Though her résumé is exemplary she cannot bring herself to work in another office. She studies every space for the quickest route to the ground outside. She takes yoga classes and calls home to learn about meditation. She assumes a new temporality. The future is a closed portal. She spends the entirety of her waking hours online, researching the many burgeoning computer modeling systems that predict future catastrophes in order to avert them, thereby securing an abundance of alternative futures, most of which are only ever theoretical. Over several months, the eventualities of climate disaster become increasingly severe while the probability of a national anthrax epidemic diminishes. Her savings approach zero less than a year after Brad and several thousand others turn to ash in the sky. Life becomes a series of disappearances. There is no horizon delineating the space she occupies. At some point she cannot stay in Manhattan. She works for two weeks in a noodle restaurant, then acquires a sales job of humiliatingly low stakes at a textile factory in Greenpoint. She sold all her business suits long ago. She takes orders from a desk in a room she shares with three other people: the floor manager, the sales lead, and the CEO. Frequently, she glances through the long window opening onto the sewing room floor. It holds five rows of five sewers each. Twenty-two of the twenty-five workers look like her mother. They hunch over their machines, swiping fabric off a pile and running it under the needles. Their hands flow smoothly away from their bodies. Itsumi does not like the chugging repetitions of the machines, which segment and distort the fluidity of the ladies' arms. She cannot explain why this bothers her.

Every night she stops at an Irish pub and drinks one glass of house red. She measures time in bartenders; none seem to work there longer than a month. More and more frequently, young whites appear in the neighborhood. One day house-made pickles and ketchup appear on the menu, an increasing selection of cocktails with exotic ingredients and hand-chipped ice. For no apparent reason, she decides one night to drink a beer instead of wine. She goes home, boils a packet of supermarket ramen, and searches the television for something she has never seen. After some time surfing channels, she stops on an antenna station that plays old movies. Tonight they're broadcasting a black and white Western. She isn't sure which one it is, but she recognizes John Wayne and one of the secondary characters [she looks him up later: Ward Bond, whom she remembers she had once seen in *The Searchers* years ago]. When the station returns from commercial, a voiceover and break-bumper identifies the film as *Hondo*. She watches until the credits finish, accepting the intermittent two-minute ad breaks every half hour or so, because it is manifestly clear to her that the commercials are part of the production. She herself is part of the production. The film requires an audience isolated on a massive scale. That's the point of broadcasting things on television. The story always exists on multiple planes. Each is a micro environment within a larger system of making and consuming. The screen is merely a central node. The ads blend seamlessly into the movie's narrative, they are messages from the same source, she blends into the heterogenous matrix of signs and images, they all cohere into a wider microcosm of her disbanded epoch. She carries dispersal with her. Every day at the factory, every night when she rents and eventually streams a Western she has not yet seen. She works through all of the Italians, Carnimeo, Colizzi, Leone… She watches every one of John Ford's talkies and silent features, going so far as to search for his lost body of work, which is of course a failure… She even dips into the exploitation flicks, some American, many German, where little people ride mock-heroically into sunsets on Shetland ponies, or black sheriffs use the authority of their badges to achieve vengeance on white frontier towns for centuries of transatlantic enslavement… The movies blend with her and she with them. Cinematic images reproduce themselves through her ordinary activities. She finds online communities of likeminded obsessives. Her consumption branches into different media, anything representing the Old West. She collects posters and photographs, maps of early rail lines, dioramas of iconic cowboy moments, vinyl records, CDs, digital music files, decorated cakes and their associated toppers, miscellaneous assortments of chintz and knick-knacks, objects alleged to have once functioned as movie props… She becomes a self-trained expert on wasteland symbologies. She develops the beginnings of a total theory of the world having to do with nuclear fission, the so-called *opening of the west*, and ancient poetic depictions of desert vagrancy. She comes to believe the salt flats in western Utah and eastern Nevada are the roving center of the cosmos that transcends functionality, a notion fed by her time on an increasingly small set of online forums and image boards, where she scours the separate parts of the constantly updating manifesto titled *introduction to post-politics* by a user named Pancho and the many commentaries they inspire. She comes to view her existence as the enactment of a half-state, something between life and death. During one of their conversations, Itsumi's mother makes reference to her longstanding survivor's guilt.

[24]

During the last Ice Age, about 15,000 years ago, Lake Bonneville was the size of Lake Michigan. It covered one-third of present day Utah and parts of neighboring states. You can see traces of the shorelines, representing different levels of the receding lake, etched into the mountains surrounding the salt flats.

Utah Travel Bureau [utah.com/bonneville-salt-flats]

[25]

Maintenance on The Pond seems long overdue. This maintenance operation could be treated in terms of art, as a "mud extraction sculpture." A documentary treatment with the aid of film or photographs would turn the maintenance into a physical dialectic. The mud could be deposited on a site in the city that needs "fill." The transportation of mud could be followed from point of extraction to point of deposition. A consciousness of mud and the realms of sedimentation is necessary in order to understand the landscape as it exists. The magnitude of geological change is still with us, just as it was millions of years ago.

Smithson, regarding Central Park

[26]

Her online wanderings carry her to uncanny locales. She conducts cursory research on the probabilities and contributing factors of certain chronic diseases—cancers of the blood, skin, and soft tissues, nodules and adenomas on the thyroid, Alzheimer's Disease and other forms of degenerative forgetting. After the fact she cannot recall how she went from one thing to another. She reads of a Marine killed in the battle of Tarawa whose remains were declared unrecoverable in 1949. After the battle, a fellow soldier reported seeing the dead man buried in a mass grave, a claim that was filed in the official record gathered by the Defense Department. The family and numerous advocacy groups hoped for decades that he would be returned. It was not until 2019 that his bones were found and identified through the use of cadaver dogs and radiographic imaging, forty years after his mother passed without satisfaction. Nearly eighty years after the war ended, locals and visitors to the island still report the occasional appearance of bones, hand grenades, and other artifacts that push through the sands. The grains wash away, and there is a mandible, a finger, a rib. News reports like this one are easy to find. Many soldiers are lost far from home. She wonders how many dead bodies exist in some unrecovered form. Is the dust she breathes the fundamental image of the world? Somehow she comes to a news item about a petrified dog carcass discovered in the melting permafrost of the northern Urals. Global climate change is causing massive thaws in previously frozen places, revealing an increasing number of ancient specimens. The dog, a puppy, is 18,000 years old. It still has a nose, claws, eyelashes, nearly all of its fur. Due to relevant data, archaeologists safely conclude it was a male. The article includes a photograph in which someone has pulled back the puppy's lower lip to display its teeth, yellower and shorter than Itsumi would have guessed, as if showing the creature for a prize at the state fair. She clicks back into a different browsing tab and learns the soldier had two brothers. One of them also died in the war. This brother's body was recoverable and so brought home to Bountiful, Utah for internment. The third brother was too young to enlist, so he stayed at home and grew old. In some ways one might call him a survivor, even though he did not fight in the war. Ever since, he could not speak of the two great losses of his life. She clicks a link to an expose about the future threat of superbacteria that remain dormant in the frozen regions of the planet. The human immune system is not evolved to fight these organisms. She types the word *survivor* into the search bar. Several million results come to her in a quarter of a second. Most are related to the American reality television series of that name. She hesitates for several moments in darkness, the screen lighting her slumped body and refreshing in her irises, before closing the browser. She forgets most of the things she has read almost instantly. Her research seems to contribute to the destruction of knowledge. Facts and data gather around a widening, empty center. She encounters a deep absence, then looks away.

[27]

One day as I was resting in the shade Mr. Muir [John Muir a.k.a. John of the Mountains or the Father of National Parks; Scottish-American naturalist, glaciologist, and early conservationist; Co-founder of the Sierra Club; author of many books chronicling his adventures in nature; "one of the patron saints of twentieth-century American environmental activity"; credited as creator of many categories which commonly define human relation to the natural world] overtook me on the trail and began to chat in that friendly way in which he delights to talk with everyone he meets. I said to him: "Mr. Muir, someone told me you did not approve of the word 'hike.' Is that so?" His blue eyes flashed, and with his Scotch accent he replied:

Hiking—I don't like either the word or the thing. People ought to saunter in the mountains—not hike! Do you know the origin of that word "saunter?" It's a beautiful word. Away back in the Middle Ages people used to go on pilgrimages to the Holy Land, and when people in the villages through which they passed asked where they were going, they would reply, "A la sainte terre," "To the Holy Land." And so they became known as sainte-terre-ers or saunterers. Now these mountains are our Holy Land, and we ought to saunter through them reverently, not "hike" through them.

Albert Palmer, *The Mountain Trail and its Message*

[28]

SFZero: An interface for San Francisco. That is to say, a new representation for the data that's already there. Your mind is full of /inaccurate/ representations that are affecting the way you use the San Francisco dataflow: steering you away from interaction and collaboration and towards unproductive reflexive data loops (forNext). SFZero designers are working double-shifts to engineer this next-generation interface that will bring you together with your cohabitants to experience the freedom that is /hard-coded/ into San Francisco's protocol.

sf0.org

[29]

Though he has a room all the way out in Bay Point, Pancho has become accustomed to long walks through the city. He'll spend all day at the machine, where his motions and thoughts are regulated by the layout of the sewing room, the mechanical repetitions of his gestures, and the task assigned to him in exchange for his more or less diligent labor, sewing together segments of certified organic cotton canvas in the manufacture of high end artisanal tote bags. He initially started walking as a way of getting exercise after work, because hours of sitting would cause his legs to cramp and his heart to stagnate, and he believed that he could feel all the blood in his body diverting to the tips of his fingers or pooling at the bottoms of his feet. He also found that he had to go well off the Caltrain route if he wanted to drink at an establishment that wasn't geared toward the parasitic torrents of yuppie technologists and Cyberlibertarians taking over the Bay Area. He would walk for an hour or two, drink to the edge of blacking out, and walk himself back into cognizance. Usually he would not sleep. Days passed this way—suturing panels of canvas, crossing beneath interstates on foot, drinking himself into a state of semi-consciousness, and somehow finding his way back.

Jean Baudrillard said that simulation was the predominant condition of the late twentieth century. He wrote of the *desert of the real*, which refers to a social reality evacuated of the real itself. Las Vegas exists to deceive the population: it is so unreal as to make its equally fraudulent surroundings seem ordinary and genuine in comparison. Its lights flash atop the supposedly lifeless sand. He wrote a book called *America* in which he reenacted Tocqueville's anthropological journey across the United States. He danced in a nightclub and speculated on American vanishing points.

In the beginning, Pancho's walks took him from the Central Waterfront [where the textile factory is located] past the façades of brick warehouses that he sometimes associated with disused airplane hangars or Hollywood movie sets, into Potrero Hill and Mission Bay where seemingly endless successions of Victorian row houses lined the streets, their repetitive similarity often disorienting him and soliciting a nebulous panic, until the row houses abruptly disappeared and his view filled with the same warehouses, demolition sites, and hybrid skeletons of wood and concrete that would become new or refurbished luxury housing complexes near the factory.

His life quickly became a layering of striations. Every sidewalk constituted a movement within a field of crossing vectors. To walk was to enter the entanglements of history and urban geography, the many constructions and demolitions that constitute and spatialize the time of cities. After a week his route expanded. He passed under the 280 and the 101, drifting into the Mission District, up to Soma, over to China Basin, and down again to the Central Waterfront as the concrete summoned.

Manning's, his regular bar, appeared out of the fog one night in Outer Sunset. The apparently spontaneous emergence of the corner building, a little brick structure with a decorated parapet and pedimented windows dating from the 1920's that now housed a café on the ground floor and a music shop above, caught him off guard and reminded him momentarily of the massive barges he would watch pull into Tacoma harbor on hazy autumn afternoons. This association itself sparked a memory of a painting he had once known in which a weary caravan wended its way out of mountainous sand dunes toward the bustling markets of a great city, suggested far back on the canvas by a gathering of faint smudges variously white, taupe, orange, and red. He would often think of this painting when watching the ships slowly drift toward the piers. The painting hung between bookcases in his father's study in a house he had not thought of for many years, so long that he hardly believed he had ever lived in it. For reasons beyond his grasp, he could not remember the house in any detail except for the study, a center of gravity that attracted him as a boy and that he realized was still exerting its influence as he circled the wharves, streets, and alleyways of San Francisco. The study, he remembered, was twenty feet by twenty feet, inset with bookcases lined uniformly with volumes bound in burgundy leather along the north and south walls. He entered from a set of double doors on the west, from which he peered straight across the room, over a lacquered bureau plat, through a large bay window radiating light onto the two wingtip chairs that framed it. It took some time for his eyes to adjust to the odd play of light, shadow, and dust. Outside, the image of heirloom roses and the long sloping yard resolved, and he imagined the hands that planted the original rose bushes nearly a century earlier, the many hands that replanted and maintained them since, over and over again, like in a film strip continuously rewound to its beginning and played through only to be rewound once more. His father's large oak desk swelled beneath the caravan painting. The surface of the desk had always been meticulously arranged with many items. A thin stack of blotting paper centered the arrangement, secured to the writing pad beneath by gold brackets etched with a dizzying mandala in which he would frequently lose himself by staring into the unmoving yet active center. Behind the pad [from the perspective of the person sitting at the desk, where, it occurred to him now, Pancho would dwell whenever the house was empty and there was no one to discover and punish him for infringing on his father's property] rested an inkwell fashioned of malachite and ormolu, on which the craftsman had mounted a golden greyhound precisely between the two crystal flutes his father kept full almost to the lip with black ink. The hound's posture suggested rapid movement, its hind leg arced as if it was about to rise and spring toward whatever stimulus had caused it to perk its ears and lift its snout into the air. Pancho recalled, he thought, that the study was always filled with lingering smoke from his father's pipe, and that he had imagined the dog was perhaps sniffing these lingering exhalations embedded in the surfaces of the room. In his memory the man was never actually in the study. He had always just breathed out, packed the pipe in its malachite box that Pancho now figured must have been of a set with the inkwell, and left. The study, as it unfolded in his memory, seemed to have been an amalgam of indistinctly symbolic objects whose force, if such a force existed, would always remain mysterious to him. On the floor beside the desk was a globe approximately two feet in diameter, cradled in a gleaming Indian-almond wood stand. Its surface was uniformly flat and printed with a picture of the world he found only vaguely familiar due to the misshapen territories and Latin words positioned across it. Years later, when assembling his manifesto, the same map reappeared online, though now in a series of a dozen framed images segmenting the world into a collage of separately represented zones. According to the description on the Library of Congress website, it was the seminal map of German cartographer Martin Waldseemüller, the *Universalis cosmographia secundum Ptholomaei traditionem et Americi Vespucii aliorü que lustrationes*, published in 1507, the first known cartographic document to use the word "America" in reference to the New World. He could never locate his home on that globe. He turned it thousands of times in those years, which in retrospect were astonishingly short, his slightly curved index finger tracing an invisible coil from south to north. Again and again it spun around its locked axis. He recognized Asia, Africa, and Europe by shape and location. To the left of Europe, assuming the typical vertical orientation familiar to American eyes, North and South America drifted in the ocean with the undeveloped contours of an embryo. They seemed like incipient, dysfunctional creatures bound for extinction, though not before passing something of themselves on to each subsequent representation of the western hemisphere, up to and including the recognizable land masses now routinely photographed by sophisticated imaging satellites. He felt as if he were a paleontologist uncovering the petrified traces of a world long vanished, filling the chasm between these primitive landmasses and those of modern cartography with all intervening varieties. He imagined that the Americas had literally expanded over time. While envisioning this territorial genealogy, a nascent fear emerged somewhere in the distance between the fixed lines of the globe and the reality of geological flux—suddenly, in the midst of his post-political undertaking, every map seemed to chart the universal certainty that everything will become otherwise, that the inconceivable majority of changes occur on scales beyond the horizon of human sense, the microscopic and cosmological sublime flowing one into the other.

Now, he edges between wakefulness and dreaming. This is the paradigm of his life, he sleeps at the machine while over and over his hands reach out, run sheets of canvas beneath the plunging needle, and set the conjoined pieces in a growing stack that the lady next to him folds, cuts, glues, and rivets. The accumulating textiles signal for him the time stolen by this work. He no longer knows why he pays rent, so he stops. His purpose is to disobey time, to exist temporarily wherever he goes—an exhalation in the form of a human male.

[30]

What is complex about contagions is that they are always multiple. A frenetic contagion of garment-making can coexist with the quietness of an experience of red turning to yellow. These are independent events occurring within a wider event-space. They are contemporary but dissociated. And yet, when the conditions allow it, they can share a feeling-tone. This vector that can activate across contemporarily independent occasions fashions a wider tonality that can begin to modulate the time of the event as a whole. Activated by vectors that cross and thus co-compose, the event has created its own mobility, its own ambiance, and in so doing, it has begun to run itself: a mobile architecture. Feeling-tones are not about ease, or about comfort. They are about the force of an individuation that momentarily refuses its own capture.

Erin Manning, "Mindfulness," *The Nonhuman Turn*

[31]

Pancho descends a flight of stairs lit red by the neon Budweiser sign in a window centering a heavy wooden door. He wades into the dark and mostly empty interior, narrower and deeper than he had implicitly assumed. He rubs his eyes and allows his pupils time to dilate, feeling as if he has stepped into an alien reality. He notices chairs stacked on the tables near the rear wall, maybe because the night is slow, or perhaps a residual trace of work completed on some earlier evening.

The bartender, bowing slightly forward as he pours whiskey into a dusty glass tumbler, services a single patron beneath the slow croon of a country western song Pancho has never heard before. The patron grumbles a command that he not stop until the liquor spills over. Of course, the bartender says. But maybe Sir would like to finish his shot before receiving more. For a moment, Pancho thinks the patron has fallen asleep. The man, whose immense body engulfs the shadows at the end of the bar, sways sideways on the stool, his chin nestled snugly in its own fat.

You, peckerwood, the patron says, reaching out toward Pancho, pointing at him, staring down his arm with his head cocked and one eye closed. Drink this for me.

The beam of a hanging bar light illuminates the side of his face in white, orange, and red radiating from a stained-glass shade. The silver ring on his pinky finger glints as he forgets or possibly disregards his own command, takes the glass for himself, and slugs the shot down. Pancho bellies up next to him. He can't figure the song playing on repeat. The patron orders drinks for them both. They clink tumblers and imbibe. After a while Pancho asks about the patron's accent. Not once does he see the man's face in whole. He is a Texan far from home. The more they drink the more they both unspool.

Pancho himself falls in and out of sleep. The first time he comes to, the patron is in the midst of explaining some old mayor's tendency of drinking here with Chinese immigrants. West and East were linked right here, in the exact spot Pancho was sitting at. That mayor grew up someplace back east, Boston or Brooklyn, some B-place [Pancho can't remember], and knew Walt Whitman when the poet was old and dying of pleuritis, whichever place Whitman came from that's where the old mayor came from, too, the guy who turned San Francisco from a forgettable little boomtown on temporary stilts into a concrete city of the future. Because of this fact, the mayor's acquaintance with the Father of American Poetry [he delivered milk to him, or ice], all the beats drank here, Ginsburg and Cassidy and Kerouac and sometimes even to this day Lawrence Ferlinghetti will shuffle his old bones through that door and tilt one back in honor of the king in the corner, the patron says, in fact the brittle corpse was here yesterday for a while until the wind blew him back out to the street, the patron drank with those uninhibited cocksuckers since the sixties and hasn't found better company since.

When Pancho wakes again, the patron is leaning far back in the shadows. The bartender's feet are visible through the window, he smokes a cigarette at the top of the stairs outside. The patron has been waiting. His talk is serious and solemn, his voice is a low croak. Every word comes out perfectly enunciated. Pancho wonders how long he has been passed out, whether the patron has sobered up or summoned an inner clarity or if he has been called to stand forth by a daemon that has entered and animated his unfolding vacancies. This building is a vestigial structure indicating a convoluted node within the weavings of global capitalism. It crosses time through simple endurance. It is the soul disentangled from the body, the body with the life excised. California ain't part of the mainland, it wasn't back in 1850. It wasn't until the trade and transportation routes developed that it really joined the Union. It still hasn't in some ways. Fruits and nuts, they say. Go out there and take a look at those people shitting in doorways, then estimate the millions it would cost to buy a room in any of the houses packed along our streets—which is to say, the millions it would cost to have someone shit on your front step. Our history is one of a grand asylum. All the obsessives and dreaming paranoids come down through the mountains or wash up on our shores and lock themselves inside. This has held firm from the dust-caked gold diggers to the hacks in Hollywood to the technocratic lunatics now quantifying and selling our existence for profit. Even Lewis and Clark were a bit delirious—they saw California everywhere they trod—and they caught it from Jefferson. We are seated within a screaming witness to an essential cosmology. History shrieks from every surface we touch. This little shit hole bar [the bartender enters, stinking of his own breath] is a center of power exceeded by the forces it set into motion. The codes of our existence are written here, because the city is pregnant with them. This is the hypocenter in every sense, ground zero for the problems of our century. San Francisco could be the first point of the American empire struck by an intercontinental ballistic missile if the North Koreans ever acquire the nuclear proficiency or the daring or the sheer madness this place attracts. The dust is waiting to liberate from its stabilized forms. This is only a temporary order. Think of the rock quarries shattered into fine powder, mixed with water and coagulating agents, and raised toward the sun to harden. Our buildings needle in vertical lines, but their reality is of the circle.

The patron claims to speak in parables, like Christ, that only the initiated can understand, so when he asks whether

Pancho does [*You know what I mean?* is how he says it, and Pancho works to hold back tears, involuntarily recalling his father's study and the county in Washington state named for his influential forebears, titans of intercontinental shipping, and trying to remember his adolescent years which, like Townes (the soft voice backgrounding the patron's speech), he had spent in the cold, lonesome room of a psychiatric ward that still in some way encloses him], the lowly saunterer, this elected reprobate either exiting or journeying deeper into his intoxication, says yes, of course he understands. Next thing he knows, he's kissing the patron's fingers. The bartender gives them another, this one gratis.

When Pancho regains consciousness, his feet are bare. He does not wear shoes ever again. He later recalls this first encounter with Manning's during a walk through Bayview Park, gazing down from the tree-filled overlook at the expanse of dirt where Candlestick Park stood for nearly sixty years, cleared and dragged smooth after the stadium was demolished between February and September of 2015. A main conveyance artery and several sloping tributaries criss-cross the lot between empty staging areas used to park heavy machinery when needed for projects in the surrounding neighborhoods; the demolition zone serves an essentially identical function as the thousands of acres of asphalt lot that had sprawled across the area when the stadium was in use. Now, in darkness, the flattened gravel resembles a piece of stretched canvas obscured by the accumulating inscriptions of an insane documentarian whose only idea is to write the page into blackness—a surface composed of the marks left on it. Beyond, the bay is a deep emptiness defined by thin glimmerings far away on the other side, and by the faint light of a single fishing boat idling in the middle.

[32]

Of his most famous work, Robert Smithson says [tangentially, in the language of gallery placards]: *The title GYROSTASIS refers to a branch of physics that deals with rotating bodies, and their tendency to maintain their equilibrium. The work is a standing triangulated spiral. When I made the sculpture I was thinking of mapping procedures that refer to the planet Earth. One could consider it as a crystalized fragment of a gyroscopic rotation, or as an abstract three dimensional map that points to the SPIRAL JETTY, 1970 in the Great Salt Lake, Utah. GYROSTASIS is relational, and should not be considered as an isolated object.*

[33]

Itsumi's eyes glaze for hours at a time over many consecutive shifts as she stares at the sewing women through her reflection in the plate glass window. It's her lunch break. She lights a cigarette, a recently acquired habit, and steps through the door. The machines roar. Every day, she tries to consume a whole cigarette with a single breath. She gets better at this, forcing the smoke to unroll inside her lungs, rotating there like a satellite that has drifted far from its orbit, unrecoverable, until the volume becomes an opaque density presaging her transition to glass. She stands there as a hardened thing, subsumed by the racket of the machines. The noise sutures and separates her, her disappearance exists before it is completed. She flickers in and out. This is activity as such, production and logistics as such. She hears the sound of the ancient loom, the tapestries Penelope burns each night waiting for her husband, inevitably, to return.

The sales manager, the third person to occupy the position since Itsumi was hired, tells her about his previous job at a meat processing plant somewhere on the edge of Queens. He can't get the smell of pigs off his clothes, even the new items he purchases. No one else ever notices it, he says, so maybe it isn't real. But I can't get rid of it. Even the textiles here stink of rendered flesh. Itsumi is somewhere far away. She fixates on the multiple nuances of tone composing his voice, as if this will bring her back. She spends so much time alone. She has trouble concentrating. She wonders whether her life is actually happening, nearly all of it passes without witness, her living is an unobserved phenomenon. Each night, she re-reads the exegeses of username Pancho's manifesto that she has written and posted over several months, which, along with the many other tracts that have accumulated across time and media, form an exoskeleton for the manifesto itself. Whether it adds anything new—any insight, any refinement of essential propositions—whether it contributes in the slightest to the functionality of Pancho's theories, every adhesion draws a wider circle around this burgeoning conceptual terrain. She enters her writings, looking deeply into the arrangements of marks the way one might analyze a segment of Proterozoic rock for the first animal traces. At the end of the week, she thickens into her routine. Boiled ramen, six long neck bottles of Lone Star, a streamed Western. Tonight it's *The Covered Wagon*, a 1923 silent feature from Paramount Pictures, an early product of the studio system widely hailed as the first big budget Western film. The climactic buffalo hunt was an accomplishment of choreography and management shot on Antelope Island, Utah, an hour or so east of the salt flats. The movie was given to her by the streaming platform's secret algorithm. It knows her. She could not explain how it works if someone strapped a bomb to her torso and demanded she do so or explode, she cannot tell whether she is killing or exhuming herself. She spends the night online, like every night, refining her theories and axioms of waste, drifting into errancy. A few stars emerge from the dripping gauze of urban light polluting the city's lower atmosphere. Her pupils must adjust when she looks at them.

No one really notices that she is missing until three weeks have passed. Another sales manager starts at the factory without ever meeting her. To him, *Itsumi* is an empty sound falling apart in space. The CEO is old fashioned and inept and cannot distinguish her from the ladies who sew. Her landlord pounds at the door, he yells her name and that her rent is late. He yanks a heavy key ring off his belt but finds the apartment unlocked. All her possessions stand in place. Her key hangs on a hook by the door, gravity is perhaps visible in the tip.

Maybe some shoes are missing. The only notable sight is his blurry reflection in the television screen. He feels as if looking at himself this way for too long might drive him insane. The room is lived in and disturbed by the movements of regimen, it seems extraordinary that it could exist unoccupied. He wonders if she is hiding in some secret bunker withheld from him, or if she is standing somewhere he simply has not thought to look, some hatch in the building concealed for the express purpose of bewildering plebeian slumlords. But it's true. The room has become a diorama of sorts.

[34]

The desert is an ecosystem with a logic of sustainability, of orientation, unique unto itself. For example, if the barrel cactus, known otherwise as the compass cactus, stockpiles moisture, it also affords direction. As clear as an arrow or a constellation, it leans south. Orient yourself by this mainstay or by flowering plants that, growing toward the sun, face south in the Northern Hemisphere.

Electronic Disturbance Theater 2.0/b.a.n.g. lab, *The Transborder Immigrant Tool* [http://collection.eliterature.org/3/works/ transborder-immigrant-tool/transborder-immigrant-tool.pdf]

[35]

Has Passaic replaced Rome as The Eternal City? Robert Smithson asks. *If certain cities of the world were placed end to end in a straight line according to size, starting with Rome, where would Passaic be in that impossible progression? Each city would be a three-dimensional mirror that would reflect the next city into existence. The limits of eternity seem to contain such nefarious ideas.*

His journey ends in a sandbox. The lowering sunlight goldens its many grains. The Instamatic sees in it a map of the earth, in the entirety of its geological magnitude; he sees, like Herodotus, the dissolution of empires, a map of forgetfulness. Oddly, he recalls the opening passage of the Aldiss novel, *Earthworks*, and softens into the appeal of the suburban sunset. The feeling is ephemeral and turns toward bones and rocks pulverized by the doings of instruments and time; deposits left after the oceans have dried and the forests have disappeared and no space remains into which a living creature might tread and dwell. He stands in the fabricated verdancy of the city park watching the far edge of the planet roll beneath the sun. A lawnmower coughs and starts somewhere in the distance behind him. Eventually the sun bleeds out, thinning to a horizontal trace enclosed above and below by layers of blackening blue. His pupils widen. A breeze acts upon an empty swing, sketching a tiny arc forward and back, forward and back…

…all sense of reality was gone. In its place had come deep-seated illusions, absence of pupillary reactions to light, absence of knee reaction—symptoms all of progressive cerebral meningitis: the blanketing of the brain…

[Louis Sullivan, "one of the greatest of all architects," quoted in Michel Butor's *Mobile*, quoted in Robert Smithson's "A Tour of the Monuments of Passaic"]

Smithson dies seven years later in a desert explosion. Does he recall this sandbox, an image of home, when his plane falls from the air? Does he contemplate duration in his approach to zero, that final burst of heat and light? Before the earth turns completely away from the sun, he imagines an experiment in which the sandbox is divided into two unpartitioned segments, one holding black grains and the other white. If a child were to run in clockwise circles, the sands would mix. If she were to run in counter-clockwise circles, not only would the colors fail to separate, they would mix to an even greater degree. This thought experiment, he believes, is proof of the irreversibility of entropy and eternity.

If we filmed such an experiment we could prove the reversibility of eternity by showing the film backwards, but then sooner or later the film itself would crumble or get lost and enter the state of irreversibility. Somehow this suggests that the cinema offers an illusive or temporary escape from physical dissolution. The false immortality of the film gives the viewer an illusion of control over eternity—but "the superstars" are fading.

Hence the significance of the flash.

[36]

Where did Itsumi go?
Many places. The Flying J Travel Center at the intersection of Interstate 80 and State Highway 31 near Omaha, Nebraska. She wanders up and down the aisles, merging with the appearance and disappearance of travelers and the things she touches. She is a drifting particle making contact with external flows. She becomes something new at every point.

What does she touch?
Motor oil; funnels; insect repellant; jerky; powered donuts; sunflower seeds; granola bars; candy of a wide and modulating variety [pink labeling is the great stabilizer]; stacks of foam coffee cups [12 oz., 18 oz., and jumbo 24 oz.] inserted horizontally into six spring-loaded tubular dispensers at the rear beverage station beneath two perpetually almost-empty baskets of individual creamers and a line of commercial percolators; the dispensers, baskets, and percolators themselves; the wall of refrigerators containing soft drinks, cold sandwiches, and individual cans of 3.2 beer; the plexiglass rack of souvenir coffee mugs, shot glasses, and postcards printed with corn fields and the Union Pacific logo; a great pyramid of Sea Queen Alaskan Salmon; the *seat yourself* sign in the attached Cinnabon; the hot food counter where patrons gaze into a glass banquet of fried chicken products, potato wedges, soups of the day and week, and macaroni salad before making their purchase, consuming their bounty, and vanishing into the glaciated light beyond the sliding doors; etc.

Why does she do this?
Every item at some point comes off the shelf. There is no day or night here, the place is always open. Time is marked

in segments of labor [the morning, daytime, and graveyard shifts] and the predictable waxing and waning of commerce, positively correlated with interstate traffic flows. Longer arcs bear out in the return and departure of clerks.

Where does Itsumi go?
West. Across grasslands and mountains and desert. Through a forest both sundry and monolithic, always very dark. To the ocean.

How did she arrive here?
She bused, hitchhiked, and walked. She could not stand still for fear of total disappearance. She does not remember the specific route she took, but she can imagine it.

Where does Itsumi go?
Berkeley. Her mother's and father's house. It is no longer home. Her life in California mirrors her life in New York. She wanders the internet, gazes in front of image boards and discussion forums. She has her say, she leaves a record of herself in the form of oblique and shadowy comments that collectively form a disbanded enterprise, a fragmented theory of codes, semblances, and waste spaces distributed across many websites. She thinks of each scrap as a footprint, or a jewel or talisman that has fallen from her pack saddle as she wends across the sands of a vast and invisible desert. One day she rides the Caltrain downtown and sets out walking. She enters dimensions of the city inaccessible by vehicle or public transportation. The streets become a mass summoning or the traces of an expanding field, the rise and fall of empires unfold in the topology of the coast. She walks for hours, day after day. Her parents might worry about her. They might wish she stayed in the house. She recalls the presence of a storage

container from one of her deep midnights. She follows the GPS to a tagged location and identifies the proper container near the shipping yards. Pancho welcomes her like a friendly shop owner. They say hello. They stare at each other. She believes he looks like a lunatic permanently imprisoned. She tells him who she is, her username, she is the other Paraboloid. His eyes turn glassy, the eyes of a fish gasping on the shore. All at once he tells her of a private investigator, a body said to be somewhere in the desert, a woman murdered by a false cowboy. We can find her, he says. There's a cash reward. The designers will pay us, even for the ring on her pinkie toe. It's all a terrible conspiracy—she's dressed in the most expensive fashion items in the world. The brand name will be read on the news every time a piece of her is found. She sacrificed herself for this. It's sheer madness. Itsumi marvels at the immensity of his prodigious collection of junk. She offers her hand. They unite and part. On the Caltrain, coasting along the bay, she ponders the secret of orbits guiding certain forms of return. She looks out at the water and the blurry vegetation along the rails. That night, she cannot sleep. She sees through the atoms of her bedroom, the city, the networks of her life. The space between them screams to be set free.

[37]

Beginning in 1940, before Pearl Harbor, scientific knowledge useful in war was pooled between the United States and Great Britain, and many priceless helps to our victories have come from that arrangement. Under that general policy the research on the atomic bomb was begun. With American and British scientists working together we entered the race of discovery against the Germans.

The United States had available the large number of scientists of distinction in the many needed areas of knowledge. It had the tremendous industrial and financial resources necessary for the project and they could be devoted to it without undue impairment of other vital war work. In the United States the laboratory work and the production plants, on which a substantial start had already been made, would be out of reach of enemy bombing, while at that time Britain was exposed to constant air attack and was still threatened with the possibility of invasion. For these reasons Prime Minister Churchill and President Roosevelt agreed that it was wise to carry on the project here. We now have two great plants and many lesser works devoted to the production of atomic power. Employment during peak construction numbered 125,000 and over 65,000 individuals are even now engaged in operating the plants. Many have worked there for two and a half years. Few know what they have been producing. They see great quantities of material going in and they see nothing coming out of those plants, for the physical size of the explosive charge is exceedingly small. We have spent two billion dollars on the greatest scientific gamble in history—and won.

The greatest marvel is not the size of the enterprise, its secrecy, nor its cost, but the achievement of scientific brains in putting together infinitely complex pieces of knowledge held by many men in different fields of science into a workable plan. And hardly less marvelous has been the capacity of industry to design, and of labor to operate, the machines and methods to do things never done before so that the brain child of many minds came forth in physical shape and performed as it was supposed to do. It is doubtful if such another combination could be got together in the world. What has been done is the greatest achievement of organized science in history. It was done under high pressure and without failure.

The fact that we can release atomic energy ushers in a new era in man's understanding of nature's forces. I shall make further recommendations to the Congress as to how atomic power can become a powerful and forceful influence towards the maintenance of world peace.

Harry S. Truman, Statement Announcing the Use of the A-Bomb at Hiroshima, Hiroshima Prefecture, Japan [https:// millercenter.org/the-presidency/presidential-speeches/august-6-1945-statement-president-announcing-use-bomb]

[38]

Where did Itsumi go?
Her phone rings one evening in 2002. She cannot raise herself from the sofa. The sun, at some point in its descent, pierces a gap in the blinds, dilating a narrow egress that closes with the passage of time. It is dark when the phone rings again. Can you hear me? her mother says. Itsumi whispers yes, her mother asks again if she can hear, she answers again curtly in the affirmative. Her father makes noises in the background. It sounds like he is moving dishes from the table to the sink or possibly the other way around. Her mother asks how she is doing and if she has moved out of the apartment yet. I worry about the empty space. I imagine you standing in a large room by yourself with nothing surrounding you and nowhere to go. I had a dream last night that you were riding a horse while the world burned behind you. I hate this thought, but it keeps returning to me. The emptiness is the most frightening part. It's almost dinner time here. Have you eaten yet? You're eating, aren't you? Yes, Itsumi says. A long pause follows. It does not occur to her that she might turn on a lamp. Six miles south, two columns of light blast resolutely upward. They are part of an installation titled *Tribute in Light*, composed of 88 searchlights mounted atop the Battery Parking Garage six blocks south of Ground Zero. The beams draw vectors linking earth and sky; migrating birds frequently get trapped in this diaphanous cathedral, mistaking the beams for solid cages, and they become like wards locked in a monumental asylum. Itsumi has not seen them for herself. She lies on her back, lifting the dial off the coffee table and holding it to her chest while her mother interviews her. She has not changed apartments yet, she finally says. Do you know of the concept of survivor's guilt? her mother asks. You can't stop living your own life. You can't just freeze in place. She proposes

that her daughter return to California, which Itsumi takes to be a suggestion that she resume the life she had stopped living long ago, it would be as if she had never met Brad in Hiroshima, never stood in the long shadows of those towers. Her father's voice comes through, both parents talk to her on speakerphone. Coming home is a privilege, he says. Another long silence. She hears him breathing. He is a taciturn man. He barely said several words to her in the weeks of her visit after the attack. When she did see him, it would be through a window pruning his rose bushes, or indirectly by the neat arrangement of the newspaper he would leave on the kitchen table each morning after reading it. He had asked her once if she would like to help him stain the deck. She had told him no, she was not in the mood for anything even minimally labor intensive. Now, he breaks the silence by coughing, a mannerism extending beyond the foggy and possibly unreal days of Itsumi's childhood. In a manner of speaking, he says, you have lost your innocence. The world as you knew it has been spoiled, it has all gone away. Yes, she says. Have I told you about the day the Americans dropped the bomb? he says. She allows her head to roll sideways, she stares at the blackened windows misted around the edges with artificial streetlight. Her jaw slackens. Her eyes reduce to shadow in their sockets. She nearly drools, swallows the saliva pooling in her cheek, and rubs her thumb and fingers together. Yes, she says. Some. Your mother says you must continue living. We will both welcome you with open arms. Consider it, please. The phone call ends. For several days Itsumi finds herself researching different modes of drift. She reads news articles and oral histories about displaced populations—refugees of the Vietnam War who piled into boats and harbored in camps across the southern Pacific with the single goal of escaping their conquered homeland and possibly ending up somewhere to live out their days; stories of a prolonged and silent epidemic of the abductions of women and girls from American Indian reservations, numbering at the time of her reading in the hundreds; a similar epidemic of missing women and girls in northern Mexico; waves of people from North African and Middle Eastern countries clinging to inflatable rafts across the ancient waters of the Mediterranean Sea, voyaging toward Spain and Italy; animal migrations permanently ruined by global climate change and other forms of human terror. How many ocean drownings? she wondered. How many deathbed hallucinations of one's early years, roving across a time and place that no longer exists? How many of the dead returned to the world as the ices recede? She reads and studies the epics of Gilgamesh and Odysseus, she wonders whether a journey toward some future point is ultimately a journey toward one's irretrievable origin, whether the task of life is to try and fail at this ultimate restoration—a method of vanishing within that unsealable gap.

More than a year later Itsumi has forgotten about this conversation entirely. One night, very late, her inbox pings with a message from her father. The subject line reads very simply, *My Life*.

I have had some difficulty beginning this message [she reads], partly because it will contain several details that I have told you about before, as well as many I have kept secret, and I'm not quite sure how I can express them with the freshness and clarity they retain every time I remember them. I have written and re-written this account many times. What you see here is my best effort to explain, and maybe even demonstrate, my sense of something for which no language exists. I hesitate even to call it "something." This something is many things, the majority of which have perhaps not found a concrete form in the world.

I was five years old on 6 August 1945. I lived with my father, Hideki, and mother, for whom you are named, and for a single month my younger brother, Genjirō, who was born on American Independence Day. Our home was a comfortable unit within a development of row houses near the piers and Prefectural Industrial Promotion Hall in the Naka Ward of Hiroshima. Father worked in a bank and had at that time recently earned a promotion to manage the major branch in the city and, with it, the large accounts of the prominent importers and exporters that drove the local economy. He was therefore able to participate in the efforts to modernize Japanese domestic life that were then sweeping all the country's urban centers. I remember portions of our home very well. For that final month, the only in which our family was complete, my mother slept in what had been my bedroom to tend to Genjirō, who woke frequently during the night. I slept on the floor beside my father's bed. He snored very loudly. Today we would likely say he suffered from sleep apnea. He would probably wear one of those complicated masks to regulate his breathing. Every morning he was groggy and irritable, but even so, I relished the manly way he would grunt and stretch his limbs, scratch himself on the ribs, and hawk phlegm into the bathroom sink so loudly that I could hear it from the bedroom, sealed off from him by the sliding door that latched by way of a tiny lever concealed in the handle. In these moments of waking, I felt as if I had a special glimpse into the mechanisms of his body, still young and marked with the traces of a muscular youth spent as a stevedore moving pallets of timber grown and harvested in the nearby countryside.

What I remember most about that house, a hybrid of old and new Japan, is Mother's elaborate rose garden. Our backyard was sunken and accessed the alleyway by a stone staircase running perpendicularly to a series of terraced flower beds that stretched from one end of the yard to the other.

Each level contained about a meter of soil that Mother had populated with different varieties of roses. I recall, I believe, a foundational stratum of pink China rose. The next level contained white and red Tea rose, then, in the middle layer, were the Red roses we are all familiar with, then another of Tea rose, and finally a topmost layer of more pink China. I still marvel at the careful symmetry of these flowery layers, a living document of the breadth and depth of Mother's mental activity when planning how the garden should appear. I cannot help but think now that she saw her maintenance of the plants as a way of tending to her own needs, and that to cultivate a garden was to cultivate the imagination from which it originated. At some point beyond my memory, she had installed a wooden trellis on the side of the house that nearly reached the tiled roof. Vines and tendrils of all varieties of rosa intertwined in their vertical wanderings, some branching off the wooden grid and attaching to the house itself. I would often gaze down on the yard from the upstairs window, enchanted by this stippling of pink, yellow, white, and red against a backdrop of green. Even the lawn was filled with luxuriant bushes, divided by narrow paths of pea gravel and black mica stepping stones. I spent many afternoons riding my tricycle through these paths that my mother had set down, hopping from one retaining wall to another, and sliding down the bannister from the alley to the garden floor. I caught dragonflies and other insects, played hide and seek with other children in the development, napped in fragrant shadows when the sun was high. Some of the plants were so tall that, as I rode, I could look up and see the enfolded heads bobbing in the westerly breezes. Even now I see the morning light filtering through their delicate tissue. This garden, this house, this development, my family, Hiroshima itself, seemed like a benevolent guardian. I was like the hero of a Greek epic.

The entirety of my being was expressed on the surface of my body. Nothing could exist unless it found solid form in the world. I was continuous with my surroundings, as were the members of my family and all Japanese people, because we were made of the same essential substance grown from the landscape. This was a space without time, a permanent hiatus from the sorrows and tribulations of the outside world. This is how I remember it. Even at the time, I think, I believed that I lived inside a splendid dream. Of course my childish view of things misled me. Little by little I learned of the horrors committed by my countrymen, the brutalities we inflicted upon our Korean and American prisoners of war (many of the former and a handful of the latter were also killed or made incurably sick by the explosion), the death marches we initiated in the Philippines, the enforced sexual slavery of women in the territories we had conquered, not to mention the widespread destruction of land and wildlife habitats that could never be restored. But none of that touched me at the time. When I think of my parents, my baby brother, and our home, all of which no longer exists, I wonder whether this phase of my life ever really happened, or if I was born into a space evacuated of all form and substance, one that I have filled over the years with images from the screen and my own daydreams, a void that disrupts the smooth continuity of my ordinary life like a desert mirage far off on the horizon.

On 5 August, my parents brought me to my Aunt's apartment in the Aki-ku Ward. She was a spinster living in the basement of a duplex at the bottom of a long valley road. The green hills were not only visible from her residence, but totally dominated the senses and the rhythms of life. One could not take a step without either ascending or descending a natural slope, nor could one drive a car except by making many wide turns along the wending path. A small creek ran behind her house. I remember once cupping my hands and drinking from it. The trees were abundant and seemed as tall and implicitly forceful as any building of the city. The whole ward felt like the other side of my childish paradise, an amplification of Mother's archetypal garden. I imagined we were all tiny insects living on the back of a friendly, much larger creature. It was easy to forget we were technically still in the city.

That night we shared a dinner of rice and fried fish. My father and his sister spoke solemnly of what to do with their mother, who they expected would soon succumb to a major illness (I never learned which). Mother joined us after she had breastfed Genjirō in the second room, where I could hear his satisfied whimpers as we ate our meal. After we had finished, Mother explained her plans for the next day: she would take Genjirō to his checkup at 8:30 and return for me later in the morning. She kissed me on the forehead. My father waved goodbye from the driver's seat. I watched their car wind up the road, disappearing behind a grassy declivity, appearing again where the road emerged from the trees, until it turned once more and I could not see it any longer.

I have imagined many times my father riding the trolley with a newspaper tucked under his arm, my mother seated in the doctor's office lounge, my baby brother swaddled in her lap. The next morning my aunt came into the second room to wake me. I think she must have been surprised to find me staring out the window. It faced west, toward the city. I only remember this detail because a low point in the hills allowed a distant and somewhat abstract view of the wharfs. The sirens had gone off earlier that morning in a false alarm. My aunt must have figured they had woken and distressed me. She sat on the thin mattress and stroked my back, reassuring me that my mother would return later in the morning and the war would be over soon. Within minutes, an American B-29 Superfortress, a new luxury line of American war implements, opened its bombing hatch and dropped the horrifically named Little Boy bomb on the city. Many sources describe the magnitude of the explosion. The detonation occurred 580 meters in the air, unfurling in an ultra-hot fireball that exceeded a million degrees Celsius at its core. Extreme heat and radiation blasted outward for hundreds of meters. In less than a minute, the surface temperature of the city reached 4,000 degrees. Tens of thousands of ordinary citizens were instantly vaporized. For many, death arrived too quickly to even register. So fast, it seems unlikely to have really happened. In a matter of seconds, all of their blood and internal organs reached a boiling point and burned through their bodies from the inside, as if recording and redeploying the fiery havoc developing around them. Their bones charred within their flesh, cooking their muscular systems until their muscles and soft tissues likewise carbonized and broke away. They were already dead when the fires consumed their remains. Friends who I met in the years since have described their own experiences. One of them, who passed away from an aggressive leukemia in 1988, had lived in a similar development to the one my family resided in, hers on the other side of the Prefectural Industrial Promotion Hall. She, her older sister, and her cousin had been gathered in the sitting room on the ground floor. Like mine, her parents were out for the morning. She never learned with certainty what their final moments were like. She told me of the shock wave that passed through their house, at once reducing it to rubble and launching each of them against the lone concrete wall that remained standing. My ears were completely useless, she told me, because the strength of the shock wave ruptured both of my ear drums. I lay on my stomach amid fragments of tile and brick, paralyzed as much by fear as by pain. Part of my clothing had completely burned away. Much of it had seared into my shoulders and legs. I bled from every point on the surface of my body. I thought I was dead. My lungs were severely burned. I almost suffocated because of the smoke and ash billowing everywhere and the extraordinary pain of crying, which caused me to cry more and thus take shallower and shallower breaths. Near my feet, I saw a hand severed from its owner's body. It was my cousin's. I could tell because it still had her wedding ring on its finger. Part of the ring had melted and merged with her flesh. My sister died instantly. Her eyes boiled in their sockets. The coagulated residue fused with the surrounding areas of her skin in a uniform formation of smoking charcoal. Half of her face had burned off her skull. My family, this friend said, existed and then it didn't. She described to me her great perplexity over the fact of her survival.

History is full of atrocities, but I cannot possibly imagine anything so sudden and devastating as what happened then. Even as the damage became clear, the sheer ferocity of suffering and destruction seemed like it could not be real. This was a world of absolute degradation, a new reality that opened up within the existing state of affairs. My friend showed great strength in telling me of her experiences. Many others have made noble efforts of preserving and disseminating the stories of the hibakusha. An early documentary titled *Children of Hiroshima* can be viewed in its entirety for free online (https://archive.org/details/childrenOfHiroshima1952). The UCLA School of Medicine, in conjunction with the university's Asian American Studies Center and the Atomic Energy Commission Laboratory, have put together a project called "Children of the Atomic Bomb," which is meant to spread awareness of the atrocities of nuclear war and, I suppose in one way or another, reactivate the terror and misery felt that August by millions so as to avert similar catastrophes in the future (http://www.aasc.ucla.edu/cab/index.html). This is a way, I guess, of staving off the detrimental effects of time.

For my part, I can tell you of the great fireball unrolling in the sky, a second sun or the seed of disaster, and the plume of radiation billowing upward from the wharfs as the bomb spread instant death across the city. In the moment, I had a perverse thought. The brightness of the flash threw me into a momentary delusion that someone was taking my picture. I actually grinned. It seemed silly. It is one of my worst memories. Equal to the memory of being thrown against the back wall of the bedroom and watching my aunt drag herself toward me with blood running down her face and hands. Equal to my return to the eradicated Naka Ward a week later, held in the arms of my father's bank associate and good friend who had been away in Kyoto on a business errand when the bomb fell. To this day, as on that one, the Prefectural Industrial Promotion Hall stands frozen in ruin, a blighted and somber monument condensing the widespread suffering of the hibakusha. Indeed, tourists can see "Hiroshima" as a localized event summarized by the steel skeleton atop the hall's obliterated dome. The hall was originally built to be a symbol of Japan's entrance into modernity. In this way, it is a ruin uniquely produced by the twentieth century. It is grotesque and humorous to me now, that tourists can pose in front of this managed portrait of the disaster. The screams, the silences, the heat and light, have all been lost.

Mr. Saito, my father's friend, apologized to me when I was seventeen years old. He felt guilty for taking me to my old neighborhood before the rubble had been cleared, a pain he had been harboring since. I panicked, he said, I held onto the absurd hope that your house would have been spared and that your parents and brother would somehow be there alive and well. I wanted you to see them and run into your mother's arms. I wanted to shake your father's hand and embrace him. I thought it would comfort you to return home. Mere days after his moment of panic, Mr. Saito took me to live with him in Kyoto, where my love of photography flourished. I spent the rest of my childhood and adolescence studying the science and techniques of picture taking. I learned the effects of natural and artificial light on the photographed object. I internalized the ideal angles for photographing a person's face in order to convey a desired emotion. I developed a preference for a specific variety of flash bulb over others making their way into the consumer market. It became my mission to document the relics of the old Japan, the shrines and temples and gardens, which are still more or less in abundance in Kyoto. By the early sixties, I had my own darkroom in the loft I rented above a convenience store near the Katsura River. The loft was very small, about half of it devoted to the darkroom. The remainder was filled with stacks of equipment and albums containing images of the idyllic remnants of a long lost Japan. I slept on a thin mat between a bookshelf and a gas hot plate. To make the place somewhat resemble home, I hung a photo of the Shintenchi market dating from the 1920s. I tried to sell my pictures first to magazines, big ones like *Life* and *National Geographic*, then to local papers and art galleries, and finally to tourists on the street, all with very little success. I suffered a chronic cough, and it made people nervous to be near me. In the years since the war, a generalized fear had developed that the survivors of the attacks incubated communicable diseases that could be spread through coughing, sneezing, and incidental forms of physical contact. I developed a chip on my shoulder against the fear and ignorance of my countrymen, which I took to be a version of the same fear and ignorance that had produced the bomb and that I feared was distorting the entire future. I watched many American war films in those days and came to see myself as John Wayne's double. I was a quiet man who harbored a great secret and sought vengeance on the growing empire in the west, and yet I cheered for him to bomb, maim, and gas his cartoonish, yellow-face enemies out of existence. I grew to hate my country as much as I hated the United States, and yet I desired both with an intensity that has yet to fully dissipate. This intensity was immanent when I met your mother, when I learned that I had been accepted to film school in the United States, when I took my post in the film and media studies department at the University of California (at the time still a very new field, developed in response to the problems raised by worldwide consumer culture and the so-called society of the spectacle), when I held you in my arms for the very first time. A doctor once told me, after I had complained of years of intense sensitivity to light and sound, that the explosion had literally burned itself into my neural pathways. My mind, and with it my very idea of reality, is branded with it in a very strict sense. My basic existence is therefore a prolonged act of memory that is at the same time very complex and very simple. To state it in plain terms, my view of the world is organized around that sudden flash. It did not occur to me in the Kyoto days that I was reenacting that original flash every time I snapped a photo of a pagoda, an orchid, or a tourist wearing a kimono. I truly believed that traveling far into the past would somehow prevent the grim future that had already unfolded. It seemed possible and not remotely foolish that I could isolate these bucolic spaces from the toxic and highly corrosive present that had built up around them, and that I could preserve them eternally in film. The return of this lost paradise was never a question to me, because

I believed that my photographs ensured it would never leave. Now, it seems as if my fear of disease, my fear of never totally recovering from the trauma of nuclear war, had diverted itself toward a desire for an imaginary past. These are two aspects of eternity, the resonating chamber between abiding presence and abiding loss. I knew my body would eventually fail me, but I was afraid that the laws of heredity would also mean the bomb still lived latently within me, and it would spread its mayhem to my children. In the early fifties, many people who thought their wounds had healed developed terrible growths all over their bodies. The government would not treat these people, but decided to subject them to scientific research instead. The results, of which the majority of hibakusha are fiercely skeptical, stated there are no long term dangers for those exposed to radioactive fallout, nor is there risk for their children. But governments lie. It has been a great fear of mine that the atrocities of the attack should resurface in the lives of my children.

I have not gone back, as you know. I have spent my adult life studying texts and images, gathering testimonies, and raking my own memory in order to develop some kind of document that might help to explain the suicidal drift of our species. Over and over again, I come to the same contradictory problem: the bomb, and everything it represents, both explains and conceals itself. It lays its power bare and in doing so confounds any reason for this power. And so I exist largely in a state of permanent drift myself. One of the problems is that I am no longer certain whether I know anything or not. After coming to the United States in 1963, I devoted most of my mental and physical efforts to forgetting about Japan. Your mother and I spoke English in the house. We took long road trips, during which I snapped photos and shot films of the desert landscapes in California, Arizona, Nevada, New

Mexico, and Utah. I wrote my dissertation on the problem of filming geological time. I did everything I could to make my mind as seemingly blank and mysterious as the desert. I believed that I was quite fortunate not to own any photographs or personal items from that house in the Naka Ward, glad that I had abandoned my albums of Kyoto and the framed picture of Shintenchi in that gloomy loft. My life, my family, and Japan itself all became abstract concepts that I shunned and replaced. Your mother decorated our little apartment in South San Francisco with stuffed trout and a ridiculous artificial bearskin rug. I worried about professional development, breathing clean mountain air, Willie Mays and the rest of the Giants, getting good gas mileage, and the specific confusion of past and future that one experiences in the desert. My life became a program of intentional displacement. Every detail supplanted an earlier version.

Your birth changed all that. Your mother and I had been trying unsuccessfully to conceive for nearly two years. Though she never said anything out loud, I was grief stricken over the thought that she believed I had been sterilized by the bomb. I could see her suspicions in the way she would lower her eyes before speaking to me, in the coldness of her fingers whenever they touched my skin. But then you came. I do not think you understand the effect you have made on my life. After your birth it became necessary for me to retrace my steps, so to speak, to revisit the seminal event of my existence, a big bang on the microcosmic level of an individual life in the twentieth century. I looked up old acquaintances, traveled to them, and recorded their stories (those still living or healthy enough to host me). I became politically active when I observed the old fears and stunted imaginations spreading through public hysteria over HIV/AIDS. I turned my camera from the big skies and open mesas of the U.S. Southwest toward the faces of survivors and their children. You know that I have done all this, but you do not know why.

I have learned that certain things have a way of coming back, sometimes after a lengthy disappearance. When the nurses brought you to me in the waiting lounge (fathers were not allowed in delivery rooms back in the seventies), I cried, as many fathers do when holding their child for the first time, but not for the usual reasons that other fathers cry. I was shocked and ultimately undone by your indisputable resemblance to my baby brother, Genjirō. You had the same pudgy chin, the same protruding ears, the same blistering wail. My old life, which suddenly felt so real that everything after it now felt like a dream, assembled instantaneously around me. I felt for the first time since I was a very small boy that I was in that house in the Naka Ward, that Mother's roses were waiting on the other side of the wall for me to seclude myself in their velvety leaves and petals. I smelled their long lost perfume. I felt their dewy heads brush my cheeks in the first light of a thirty year old morning.

That evening, as I have done on most since, I sat on the deck and watched the sun set over the faraway fishing boats gliding silently across the San Francisco Bay, confronted by the odd resemblances that can arise between distant moments of one's life. My greatest fear has been that my first family, the world we shared, and the blazing light that devoured them are nothing more than my own private creations. That evening, the small sphere of North Berkeley, our house, the calm waters in the distance, struck me as translations of that earlier period. Our new family, the place we lived, was a flickering image of the old one, on top of which it had all been superimposed, and through which the old reality was now emerging. I watched the sun transition from its golden color to a deep orange, then red, a bloody aureole spilling light from the confines of its fiery circle into the darkening atmosphere. I went inside after it fully set, stirred by a restlessness that I can only describe as the slow movements of a vague and shadowy lack. I had seen Genjirō reemerge in your newborn form. In the surface of my tea, in the transparent reflection in the window, in the solid likeness cast back to me from the bathroom mirror, I could not tell whether I was the spitting image of my mother or father, a mixture of both, or a combination of features that did not add up to any obvious progenitor. I had no pictures to compare myself to except those preserved and possibly invented by my memory. The bookshelf in our living room contained a number of atlases in addition to novels and books on the history and theory of film. I moved the ash tray and coasters to the ends of the coffee table and spread a map across its surface. The names were starkly familiar and brought with them vivid images of the old pagodas, the concrete banks of alleyway canals, the hills surrounding my aunt's semi-rural duplex, the crying bell of the streetcar, the immaculate gardens leading to the Prefectural Industrial Promotion Hall, the metallic clippings of my mother's shears, the quality of sunlight filtered through roses that was lost forever when the searing fireball split the sky, of which this night's sunset was a fading reflection. After a while (who could remember how long after so many years, given the way intense scrutiny of the past opens blank intervals in our sense of time), I heard you crying in the other room. Your mother lay in the bed beside your crib, drifting to sleep. She was comfortable at last, she whispered. She needed her rest. I entered, closed the blinds to blot out the shaft of moonlight stretching across her legs, lifted you in your blankets, and tended to your shrieking call, finally, for relief.

Eric Blix is the author of the story collection, *Physically Alarming Men*. His writing has appeared in numerous journals and anthologies, including 3:AM, Best Small Fictions, The Collagist, Western Humanities Review, and others. He is an Assistant Professor of English at Valdosta State University in Valdosta, Georgia. *The Prodigious Earth* is his first novel.

The Scourge of Villanie
John Marston

Civilisation Its Cause and Cure
Edward Carpenter